Dragon Girl

Reagan Freeman

To Moana
My sweetest kindred spirit. I miss your hugs,
your bright smile, and your contagious laugh,
until we meet again…

And

To my mom
The one who has always been there for me…

Contents

Prologue

Dragon Girl

Prologue...

"Lies!" The warlock screamed, throwing the dark glass orb that rested in his hand. The smoke inside of it slowly dispersed as it shattered against the wall. The old silver haired fortune teller sat cross legged in her faded green robe. She gazed at him calmly from her worn, ragged pillow as he filled the room with his rage. They were currently in the fortune teller's home, a small stone cottage that sat in the midst of a dense, lush forest. After many years of perfecting his power in the art of dark magic, the young warlock decided to visit the renowned fortune teller. Anything she ever said had come true. Her flawless technique was to take a glass, fill it with incense smoke, and look inside the glass to tell the future. She had been mysteriously missing for two years. When she returned, the warlock came to her; he was furious at what she told him.

"It is true," she said, unphased by his anger. "I saw your future in the glass. You will lose all you have gained unless you can find a way to restore your powers."

"But I haven't lost my powers! You must be wrong! Change it somehow!" The words raced from his lips, fuming with disgust.

"You haven't lost them, yet. There is something off about you," she paused for a brief moment, "there is a hole in your aura, and all your magic is slowly vanishing. Unless you can find a way to heal it, you will lose it all.

Even if I wanted to help you, I can only *predict* the future. I can do nothing to change it."

"How long do I have until my fate you speak of is sealed?"

The fortune teller was quiet for a minute.

"Thirteen years."

The warlock paced for a moment then turned to the old woman.

"You are no longer of any use to me."

"I hoped my vision was amiss." The woman bowed her head solemnly as the warlock pointed at her. Instantly she was gone, not leaving a single trace. The warlock faltered, staring at the empty space where she previously sat. The worn ragged pillow, still warm from her presence, sat empty. He briefly considered following her, but decided she wasn't worth it. Instead he opened a portal, and stepped through.

He emerged, out of the portal, at his home. A tall, dark, menacing castle, it loomed above the clouds and rose majestically from the side of the mountain. To build something of this magnitude would have taken decades. Impatient as he was, the warlock had chosen to use his own magic to create it. The castle was enormous; made of only precious obsidian through and through. The hallways were lined with torches that burned a deep ominous red. The torches didn't give much light or warmth, but instead threw menacing shadows on the reflective stone. There were no windows, no paintings, not even carpets. It was always cold. Silent slaves, which the warlock had acquired on his many raids, walked the halls keeping the castle in order but never interacting directly with their cruel master unless he summoned. He had taken their voice, and brought each one to their cold, dismal fate, in shackles. They either learned to serve him flawlessly, or they were never seen again.

Angry and agitated, he stormed through the lofty, barren hallways. His servants tirelessly scrambled to get out of the way before he could see them. Fortunately, he paid them no attention as he went straight to his workplace; a large room set apart specifically for improving his magic. There were shelves of potions and tables cluttered with cauldrons and books. He went straight to a shelf stocked with books. Hauntingly, he ran his hand along the spines until he saw the one he wanted. He pulled it off the shelf and opened it.

Then excitedly, he gathered a large cauldron, and ingredients for a spell. With the wave of his hand he summoned two of his servants, a boy and a girl. As if they read his mind, they brought buckets of water to the cauldron and filled it. The two lowered their heads and went to leave, but the warlock stopped the girl, and ordered her to light the fire below the cauldron. He knew he could do it himself with a snap of his fingers, but he wanted his slaves to continue serving him. They needed to continue knowing who was in charge, so he made them work whenever he could. The girl lit the wood below the pot, bowed, and left as quickly as she could.

The warlock smiled, he enjoyed the feeling of power and instilling fear. Specifically fear from his subjects. He shook his head, bringing his anger back and quickly returned to the task he had at hand. After adding the ingredients into the bubbling water, he watched as the fluid swirled. Turning different colors, the concoction glowed softly. Satisfied, he asked the question he wanted to know.

"How can I restore all my powers?"

The cauldron glowed a deep purple, the contents swirling until an image emerged. The warlock gazed at a man and woman smiling into a cradle. In the soft white bedding of the cradle laid a young, sweet baby. She gazed up at them with wide, golden eyes. He quickly recognized them as royalty by the crowns they wore and the gilded cradle. The cradle gently rocked the sweet one year old babe as she giggled at her parent's beaming faces.

"Kill the girl," a wispy voice said from the cauldron. *"Kill the girl when she is fourteen years of age and her inner magic shall be yours."* The warlock grinned and went to touch the image, but it flashed red and and his outstretched hand was burned from scalding heat.

"Aaaahhhh!" He shouted, pulling his hand back. He cursed. "If I cannot touch her, how am I supposed to kill her?"

Though he had not meant to ask the cauldron, the image quickly rippled into a new vision. This time it was a dirty woman, dressed in rags, yelling at a boy who couldn't have been more than three years old. She pointed at a broken vase, surrounded by a puddle of water, as the young boy held a reddening cheek. The wispy voice from the cauldron spoke again.

"The boy.He is weak minded and obedient. Use the boy to kill the girl. Use the boy to kill the girl." A smile stretched across the warlock's face.

"Where are they," he forcefully asked his third and final question. The image once again swirled, this time, showing a map. The warlock snarled in frustration. The map was of Acodia, a peaceful kingdom across the sea, almost a year's ride by boat.

Disgusted, the warlock slapped the liquid in the cauldron. The glowing stopped, returning the water to a murky grey. He stormed away to another shelf and took a long, slender flask into his hand. It was a dull green, the color misleading as it had a mystical power surrounding it. He grimaced, paused, then uncapped it. It was as if a part of him were being torn from his whole being as it viciously drained some of his magic from him. When he felt like he had saved enough, he recapped the flask. His weak, shaking body fell to the ground after doing so. His head spun a moment, then he slowly stood, feeling nauseated. He went to his grand bedchamber, and sat at his desk. A large book waited for him. It was opened to a blank page. He cleared his head, then his throat, and spoke.

"The cauldron said that I had to kill the girl when she was fourteen years old, thirteen years from now. By that time I will be too weak, but I will still need my powers. In preparation for this, I have carefully stored them away for the future." As the warlock spoke, the words appeared on the page, documenting what he said in his journal. The warlock stood, a wave of feebleness washing over him, he moved to his door. He opened it, and in doing so, caught a silent and startled slave off guard.

"When I return, I expect everything to be in order," was all he said before returning one more time to the book.

"Tonight I rest. Tomorrow, I board a ship to Acodia."

Chapter One

The Princess

"Coming through, watch out, sorry!!" Kara shouted as she pushed through the crowded bright hallways of the castle. She brushed against multiple servants and maids. All the while pulling straw out of her dress and running her fingers through her hair in a desperate attempt to conceal her disheveled appearance. *Oh, father is going to kill me.* She thought as she ran to the dining room. Leo ran behind her, and she heard the clanking of his armour as he struggled to weave through the crowd due to his large stature beneath the armor. When Kara was born, Leo was already 15, and training as a young knight. He had sworn to watch over her since the day she was born, promising to protect her at any cost. For the first few years of her life (when she was old enough to think for herself) she resented Leo, thinking he was simply an overprotective babysitter. But over the years, Kara realized she didn't mind, he was her best friend and never stopped her from having fun -- unless she was in danger.

Kara stopped in front of the large, solid oak door. Behind the door sat the small, private dining hall. She quickly brushed off her dress and straightened the dainty crown on the top of her messy, tangled hair. Doing her best, she elegantly entered the extravagant dining hall while Leo stood watch outside. As she entered, she glanced around the room, taking in the woven tapestries of her ancestors. Tapestries that portrayed noble men riding great horses into battle, or embarking on hunts into forests searching for terrible beasts. The largest one hung at the back of the room. It showed the king and queen holding a young child wrapped in precious, white linens. The queen stood straight, elegant, and tall. She was adorned in a brightly colored blue dress that complemented her cheery smile and light brown hair. Her skin was a rich bronzed color, and her brown amber eyes shone as she seemed to gaze out of the painting.

The queen's delicate name, Ella of Acodia, perfectly matched her exquisite and exotic beauty and grace. Memories of her mother danced across Kara's mind. Images of galloping on horseback across the plains and hills with her mother beside her danced through her mind. Her mother stealing sweets from the kitchen with her. And once even going to town in a carriage together. Even in wild, fun acts of mischief, the queen was always kind and gentle. The sweet memories of the mother she loved brought a smile to Kara's lips. But quickly the memories of their last months together sombered Kara. She remembered, all too well, the chest rattling coughing fits and the paleness of her mother's skin. Remembering how she became thinner and thinner, and her tender hands becoming so very frail. Somehow, through it all, the light in her eyes had never gone out. Kara could still hear her mother's last words. *"You, are meant for greatness, my only Kara."* The words were sweetly spoken and in the blink of an eye Kara was rushed out of the room.

Kara's mind eased back to the present as she continued to stare at the tapestry. Her father stood beside her mother in the tapestry, one hand protectively around her shoulder, and the other, under his wife's hand that held the child. He was large, bold, and young; a grand king that ruled his land as a just and strong leader. A proud smile was evident through his closely trimmed beard. Tearing her eyes from the tapestry, Kara looked to the rectangular table, made of solid dark oak,that stood in the middle of the room. The cold stone floor was covered by a beautiful rug with intricate designs placed underneath the table. Her father, the king, already sat at one end of the table, and an empty chair with a plate was placed at the other.

"You're late," the King said. He was tall and magnificent, with dark golden hair and stone grey eyes, but he was aging quickly. His strong, close trimmed beard showed strands of gray and a grim expression settled over his face. Ever since the queen died of fever several winters ago, it was rare to see him smile. Kara cleared her throat and sat down.

"Sorry father, um, geography ran long." She poked her cold chicken with one hand and twirled a piece of hair with the other. Usually she loved meat, but she was so worried, she couldn't eat.

"Geography? Strange, I heard some maids say Leo was sparring with an unknown knight down in the training fields. Isn't he supposed to stay with you at all times? Also, the dirt on your face and hay in your hair say otherwise." Kara sighed.

"I'm sorry father, but honestly, I just-"

"No Kara, I've already told you not to leave the castle grounds, or interact with the knights. What if one of them had been sick, you could've gotten sick too. Or what if someone had seen you, the princess, walking to the knight grounds, they could've taken you."

"But I didn't walk," Kara mumbled.

"What!" The king shouted. Kara immediately regretted saying that.

"Father-"

"You rode a horse?! Please tell me you didn't ride that stallion you go so often to see."

"His name is Obsidian, and even though he's a stallion, that doesn't mean that he's going to buck me off!"

"Kara!" The king said, standing up suddenly. Kara sighed, she knew what would happen next. "Go to your room, I will send your dinner later." Defeated, Kara didn't even protest, she just stood and walked out of the room. The nursemaid and Leo were standing outside the door and followed Kara up to her room.

"Because heaven forbid I'm alone for a moment!" Kara yelled to no one in particular. When she got to her room, she opened the door, stepped through, then quickly turned and slammed it in the nursemaid's face. She locked it and walked across her room to her bookshelf. She ignored the incessant knocking from her ever present two shadows, Leo and the nursemaid. She didn't read much history, even though that was all that was there, but there was one book she was fascinated by.

"The Dragon History," She read the cover aloud as she took it off the bookcase. It was a large, brown book with the title etched in black. It was old; its pages yellowed by time and the spine sadly fraying. Sometimes it was hard to read the flowing handwriting because of water blotches.

Not even water blotches could keep her from reading the book, nothing could. She had always loved myths about dragons, and since she found the huge book months ago, she couldn't get enough. Through the book, her knowledge of dragons had grown immensely. She knew that there were three subspecies of dragons that lived in Acodia. The drakes, normally just referred to as dragons in general. The drakes were grand dragons with four legs, fire resistant scales and wings, a spiked or clubbed tail, and the ability to breathe fire. Then there were filatas, dragons that were much like the drakes, but with wings feathered similarly to colorful birds, and smaller, softer scales. Instead of breathing fire, which could catch their feathers aflame, the filatas possessed the ability to charm other creatures and dragons. Finally, there were the wyverns. They were the smallest, and most ridiculed dragon species out of the three. Instead of having four legs, wyverns only had two, and in place of the front legs, were its enormous wings. It did not speak a language at all, and wyverns were known for cruelty.

Kara placed the large book down with a *thump* on the table. A small orange ribbon hung through the book, holding the place where Kara had stopped reading, she opened it there, moving the seemingly timeless shimmering ribbon out of the way. Kara smiled in anticipation, feeling a tinge of disappointment, as she saw she was on the final chapter of the book.

"Fear and anger spread throughout the land as hundreds of dragons fought one another in the skies and throughout the land, bringing destruction to Acodia. The people of Acodia were driven from every land, the dragons seemingly unaware that humans even existed. Many Acodians died as the dragon armies fought. The king pled with the surrounding countries to help, but the nations feared the powerful and numerous dragons of Acodia. They believed the war that raged in the land amongst the dragons was a sign that Acodia was cursed, so they refused any call for help. Throughout the kingdom, there was the horrid and ever present sound of steel on steel, claw on claw, and beast against powerful beast as the armoured dragons fought. It was a fight for power, for glory, and for honor. No matter how many died for the cause, neither side relented, ceaselessly fighting on and on. The death toll was innumerable, each side losing more and more of the kingdom as the war

wore on. *After many years of death, fear, and agony, the two dragon kings agreed--In order to stop the bloodshed on both sides, they would fight each other in a duel, an ancient tradition for the dragons. The victor of the duel would ascend to the title of "King of the Dragons," and the defeated king would be exiled or killed. The battle between the two dragon kings was barbaric. The ground shook, mountains trembled, and forests turned to ash as the two leaders fiercely fought to gain control. Years passed without a pause, the two enormous creatures destroying and ravaging the kingdom as they fought. At last, as both dragons began to feel the years of battle bleeding in their bones, Ranith the White struck Lusarth the Black with a thunderous clap of power. As Ranith rose high into the clouds, the black dragon fell out of the sky, defeated by his foe. Lusarth was banished, exiled -- and there was peace among the dragons. However, King Leland of Acodia was devastated. Hundreds of helpless Acodians had been killed, and many more would die of starvation. The land was scorched and barren after the battle. As he glanced at his barren land once green and lush with life, his anger increased. King Leland was furious and demanded that the dragons leave and reside in a small area north of the capital. The area was located in the outlands. Tired from years of war and battle, the dragons obeyed. The king decreed that any interaction between his subjects and the dragons was forbidden. Because of King Leland's brave actions, and stalwart determination, the kingdom of Acodia remained safe and peaceful for decades. Thus, ended the reign of the dragons.*

    Kara read the pages with wide eyes.

    "That can't be it!" She said, dismayed. A loud bang on her door, breaking the silence, made her jump.

    "Princess, are you alright?!" The anxious voice of a maid penetrated through the door.

    "I'm fine," Kara quickly shouted back.

    "You haven't been answering us."

    "I'm trying to sleep," she called again, more calmly this time.

    "But, your dinner-"

    "I don't want any tonight, now please leave." With that, and the dragons still swirling in her head, she got in bed and blew out the candle.

    In another part of the kingdom, a young, fifteen year old boy was sowing seeds in barren dirt. Nothing had grown in the dry dust for years, whether or not it rained, life refused to rise. Day after day he worked, but nothing ever grew. The boy wiped his brow, which was wet with sweat after being outside all day in the hot sun. His brown hair was matted and greasy, and he was scrawny for a boy his age.

    "Cole, are you done yet?" His mother yelled from the door of the shack they called a house.

    "Yes Mother," came his humble reply.

"About time, the sun is almost down! Get in here and get to bed, now!"

"But Mother..." he paused. "What about dinner?"

"What about dinner," she cried, her voice growing shrill. "How dare you talk back to me! I am your mother. I've worked so hard to keep you alive, and this is how you repay me. You no good maggot, do as I say!"

Cole regretted having said anything. He bowed his head in defeat, and even though his stomach rumbled in protest, he did his best to ignore it. Yet another night he would go to bed without dinner. He went into the dirty, run down house and climbed the ladder to the loft. There, his bed of boards and hay greeted him. His mother had the only bed in the house, and she was appalled by Cole enough already. Cole considered himself lucky to even get to sleep inside at night. With a sigh, he laid down and looked at the stars through the hole above his head.

He heard his mother below him open the cabinets and slam them shut. A stream of curses fell out of her mouth as she stomped around down there. Cole fought to keep his eyes open as he daydreamed about another life. He smiled, thinking of his image of a perfect life. One where he would never have to see the field, the rickety house, a hoe, or the wicked witch he called a mother ever again. A life where people admired him. A life in where he was well cared for and maybe even educated. After what seemed like forever for Cole, he finally heard his mother go to bed, cursing all the way about him. He lay still for a few minutes longer, waiting until his mother's breathing became deep, loud snores. Slowly he sat up. For a week straight, his mother had only fed him breakfast, accusing him of talking back or some other crime so she didn't have to feed him lunch or dinner.

Every night, after his mother was asleep, he would get out of bed and find something to eat. Being careful not to step on the rung that creaked on the ladder, he silently descended below. He then tiptoed to the cupboard, and opened it.

"Wha-?" He caught the word as he whispered in surprise. The cupboard was bare, not a speck. He moved to the next one, then the last. Each one was empty. His shoulders slumped as he instantly made a decision. Cole packed his few belongings, hefted his bag over his shoulder, and walked out the door into the cold night air.

Chapter Two

The Bull

The warlock watched as the boy left the house, a smile showing on his wicked lips. For thirteen years, he had watched the boy, and now he was positive the time had come. The boy walked all night, doing his best to go in the direction his mother had always gone when she had gone to the village. By the time he actually reached the village, far from his house, he was tripping over himself with weariness. He clumsily walked into the first tavern he saw and sat at the bar.

"I'd like a room and dinner please," He said, his words slurring together. The barmaid, a pretty little thing with round cheeks and long, curly hair, turned to him.

"Sure, that'll be six copper gilsar." She said with a smile. The boy was shocked. He had never had to worry about money, and the only thing he knew about it was that his mother always wanted more.

"Gilsar?" He asked. The girl kept the smile up.

"Yes, a room and breakfast aren't free, you know?" She said jokingly. The boy looked out the window and saw it was indeed morning instead of night. He faced the girl again.

"I don't have any money." He said, feeling a stone in his stomach. The girl frowned. She seemed to think for a moment, before reacting.

"Rohard," She called. A large, rough looking man with an unchecked beard walked over to her, on Cole's side of the bar.

"What?" He asked, his voice gruff.

"Rohard, this boy wants a room and a meal for free." She explained, trying to be soft and nice. The man turned to Cole.

"Get out," he said simply. Cole's jaw dropped as well as any hope he had left.

"But-" Rohard didn't let him even start. He grabbed Cole by the back of his shirt, dragged him, then threw him out the door. Cole landed hard in the dirt road, then turned and desperately tried to get back inside.

"My bag is in there," he tried to explain, but Rohard didn't care.

"If it doesn't have any money, you don't need it, now get out of here." He said, standing firm. Cole went to say something more, but he knew it was no use. He gave in and walked away, his stomach grumbling and eyelids barely staying open. He sleepily walked out of town and over to a tree, slumped against it, falling asleep almost instantly in the shade it provided.

When he woke up, the sun was high in the sky, and there was a man sitting right in front of him. He jumped and wished he hadn't, realizing just how sore he was from sleeping against a hard tree after walking and working the day before. The man looked old and frail, and was wearing a simple brown cloak. He held his bony, long hands in front of him on his lap. Cole couldn't see much of his mouth, on account that he had a full gray beard.

"Who are you," he asked the man. The man only smiled.

"You look hungry, have an apple." The man reached into his cloak sleeve and handed a shining red apple to Cole. Cole was far too hungry to worry about who the man was anymore. He took one huge bite after another, not caring as the juice dribbled down his chin.

As Cole devoured the apple, the man spoke. "To answer your question, I'm a friend. I noticed you ran away from home, and I want to help." Cole just nodded as he continued eating. "What if I told you, I could make you the king?"

Cole nearly choked at that, not knowing if he had heard the old man right.

"Me, king?" He asked, his mouth full. The man nodded.

"With a small amount of time, and a little bit of magic, I could make *you* the new king."

"Magic? You're a -- a warlock?" Cole asked in disbelief. The man nodded calmly.

"Yes, and I will now tell you how to become king. That is, if you agree." Cole nodded eagerly, seeing his future becoming instantly brighter and less hunger filled. He shook from his mind the idea that maybe he was still dreaming. The man grabbed a bottle that was tied around his neck and barely uncapped it, then clamped it shut. "Alright, I'll take care of the details, but all you have to do is marry her," he said, drawing a circle in the dirt with his finger. Once the circle was complete, an image formed. It showed a young girl in a simple riding dress, laughing as she galloped on the back of a black horse. She looked average, with untamed, wild brown hair, and a dirty face. Then, Cole noticed her eyes. Instead of regular brown or green eyes, she had bright gold eyes. Then, he noticed her horse was wearing a royal seal.

"The princess!" Cole almost shouted. The man quickly hushed him. "But I've never even seen the castle, not even from a distance! How could I ever marry her?" He asked quickly and quietly, a storm of questions coming into his mind. The man raised an eyebrow.

"How do you feel about becoming a knight?"

Less than five minutes later, Cole looked at his reflection in the lake. He was dressed in a full suit of shining silver armor lined with blue. Despite the fact that he had never seen a piece of armour, he was amazed at how great the workmanship was. Not only that, but the warlock had also made him stronger, faster, and given him an enchanted sword. Cole smiled at his heroic looking reflection, then frowned.

"I look good, but there hasn't been any need of knights for years."

The warlock smiled, uncapping the bottle once more.

"I will be back in a moment," he said, before vanishing. Cole stood there, confused, but he waited.

Far away, the warlock reappeared in the corral of a docile brown bull. Even though the bull was clearly startled, it made no movements to attack. The warlock smiled.

"You'll do." He directed both hands at the bull, muttering words under his breath. The bull watched, then started to jerk and spasm. The bull bellowed loudly as if it was in pain, but the warlock didn't stop. The bull's muscles bulged and foam dripped out of its mouth. Its dark brown coat changed from brown to white as the bull doubled in size, its horns growing to at least three feet long. The bull snorted and kicked as it continued to grow. Its eyelids snapped open, revealing a new color of furious red eyes. Its muscles bulged, and additional horns formed, creating a crown of smooth piercing spears around its head.

Finally, the warlock dropped his hands and examined the bull. It was now three times larger than it originally was, and it snorted smoke as its eyes, full of hatred, fixated on the gate of its corral. Furiously, the bull charged and broke easily through the wooden gate. The bull continued to charge until it was out of sight. The warlock smiled, feeling accomplished as the first part of his plan spun into action. Then, he cast a small curse on someone days away. He disappeared and reappeared at Cole's side.

"Now, we wait."

Kara jumped back from Leo's wooden blade, sucking her belly in so it passed inches away from her stomach. The two of them were just outside of the knight training area, and Kara was enjoying every minute of it. She was supposed to be studying history, but Leo had helped her sneak away for more sword practice. Kara smiled and rushed forward, remembering the parries, attacks, and footwork that Leo taught her. She advanced, moving her sword in unpredictable patterns, trying to get an opening, but Leo struck first, tapping the inside of her right shoulder lightly with the tip of his wooden practice sword. He smiled a little.

"You're improving," he said. Kara nodded, taking a moment to catch her breath.

"Great, let's go again." She raised her sword, but Leo shook his head.

"Aren't you having dinner with the king tonight?"

Kara's eyes widened and she looked to the sky, trying to see what time it was.

"Oh no!" She ran to Obsidian, who had been grazing the long grass not too far from where they had been practicing. She hopped on his back and kicked his sides. Obsidian started in a small trot, then accelerated to a full gallop. Kara felt the ground fly beneath her as the castle got bigger and bigger. She turned and saw Leo not too far behind her, trying to keep up on his own steed. She reached the outside of the castle walls. The entire castle was surrounded by a thick, tall, stone wall. It formed a square around the castle and the small courtyard inside. The stables were the closest thing to the wall. There was thought to be only one opening, the drawbridge, but Kara knew another way.

Frantically she looked and felt, trying to find the spot Leo taught her about. Leo had told her a few years earlier how, centuries ago, the king who ordered the building of the wall made one extra feature. In case of attack, he had always wanted to be able to get out of the castle safely, so he had a part of the wall made especially for that purpose. Years of new kings, who dismissed the wall, eventually led to the knowledge of its presence fading away. There was, however, a family whose eldest son of each generation served the king. They kept the knowledge of the secret escape, which Leo passed onto Kara.

Kara finally found the part she had been looking for and pushed against the tall and mighty wall with all her might, and then, she felt it move. Or, at least a portion. A small part of the wall, just big enough for Obsidian with her on his back to get through, swung outward. Kara breathed a sigh of relief, she waited for Leo to get through as well before pushing the wall closed and walked Obsidian into the stables. Leo took Obsidian's reins and waved Kara off, telling her to go before she was late. She silently slipped back into the castle, grateful that Leo had reminded her to leave the knight grounds when he had. Now, she had time to look presentable for her father. Dinner would be held soon. Kara rushed to her room, washed her face, and brushed her hair before picking out a fresh dress. It was a dark green, elegant dress that fell down to just inches above her feet. The sleeves ended above her elbows and were narrow. She heard her door open and saw Leo walk in. She turned to him.

"Do you think my father will ever know?" She asked, waiting for his answer. Leo looked her up and down, then walked forward. He grabbed something off her dresser, and gently placed it on her head. Kara turned to look in the mirror, and saw he placed her crown on her head. When she looked back to him, he shook his head. Kara let out a breath of relief. She knew even though Leo didn't smile and reassure her with empty comments, he believed that her father wouldn't know. Leo was just quiet, and Kara appreciated that, especially when she needed to rant.

Someone knocked on the door and announced that the king was waiting for Kara to start dinner. Kara sighed, went to the door, and followed the maid down the endless hallways. She glanced around herself, taking in the high ceilings, wide windows, and occasional paintings. When they got to the dining hall Kara was surprised to find that she was the first one in the hall.

"I thought you said that my father was waiting." Kara said to the maid, who looked just as confused as her. Just then, the king came through the door. Kara went to greet him, but stopped. Instead of his strong, purposeful stride, he was slightly bent, as if he had a weight on his shoulders. He slowly walked to his seat. Kara quietly took her seat at the other end of the table and studied her father as the servants brought out the food.

"Father, is everything alright?" She asked cautiously. The king looked at her.

"Yes, of course. It just appears that I have a non-threatening case of fever." Kara felt her heart jump. That was what her mother had said.

"I'll be fine." The king said, reassuringly, but Kara didn't believe him. The king began eating the steaming soup in front of him, but Kara had no appetite.

"May I be excused?" She asked, hoping her panic wasn't showing. The king didn't look up.

"It'll be the second night you've gone without eating dinner with me."

"I'll eat in my room." She replied numbly. The king nodded, giving her permission to leave. Kara stood, and left, knowing that a servant would bring her dinner to her room. She exited the dining hall, hearing Leo's almost silent steps follow her to her room. He patiently waited, until they were in her room, to begin asking questions.

"What happened?" He asked as soon as he closed the door. Kara numbly went to her bed and sat, mortified.

"My father has a fever," she said. Leo stayed silent, taking a moment to process the information. Then he sat by Kara on her bed and put a hand on her shoulder. With that touch, Kara broke down. She bent over and cried, letting out all her fear, frustration, and despair. Leo didn't talk, but just sat, letting her cry. After a while, Kara sat up and wiped her tears. Leo handed her a handkerchief, and finally spoke.

"You are strong, and stubborn, and you had to have gotten those traits from somewhere. If the king dies, it'll be fighting, not groveling sick in bed."

Kara wiped her red, puffy eyes and smiled. Then, she punched Leo in the shoulder.

"I'm not that stubborn."

Chapter Three

The Decision

"Your Highness! Your Highness!" Kara and her father were sitting in the throne room, her father in his grand throne of gold and Kara in her smaller one of mixed gold and silver. The king's advisor stood by his side, and Leo stood by Kara's. The pure silver throne that once was her mother's remained empty.

"What is it," Kara's father asked the sweaty and out of breath messenger boy. The boy took a moment, breathing heavily, before speaking.

"The eastern states, they're under attack." Everyone in the room gasped, including the king. For over one hundred years, there had been peace in the land.

"Who is attacking?" The king asked.

"There is a bull, rampaging across the kingdom." Everyone relaxed. "It's already taken out many large farms. It seems to be targeting medical fields and apothecaries." The king stroked his beard.

"No one has slayed this bull?"

The messenger shook his head.

"They are calling it the devil bull. It is pure white, with red eyes. It is larger than any bull anyone has ever seen, full of bulging muscles, anger, and hate. It snorts fire with smoke that rises through what appears to be a crown of piercing thorns."

Kara heard her father scoff.

"Send a few of my knights to slay it," he told the messenger.

"Yes your Highness," he replied, and left with a hint of reluctance.

"Father, do you really think the bull is white and red and snorts fire?" Kara asked.

The king scoffed again, but it developed into a rattling and nasty cough. Kara gave a concerned look to Leo, who just looked sad.

"I believe the bull is a problem, since it has attacked our suppliers of medicine, but no, I think the messenger was exaggerating to convey the urgency." The king began to cough again, but in between a cough he spoke.

"Kara, why don't you bid good luck to the knights before they leave," he said weakly. Kara swallowed and nodded, fear making her throat tight. She quickly left the room, but before the door closed, she saw her father leaning heavily on his advisor, coughing harder.

"He's getting worse," she said earnestly to Leo once they were well on their way to bid the knights farewell. "And you heard what the messenger said, the bull is taking out farms that provide medicine, you know that there are not a whole lot of those." Leo nodded, keeping a grim expression. "You don't think my father could actually..." Kara stopped, she couldn't bring herself to say it. Leo stayed silent. Collecting her thoughts, they both walked in silence.

It wasn't long until they reached the courtyard of the castle where the knights were gathered and ready to leave. There were five in all, each were dressed in full armour with the royal emblem, a strong steel sword surrounded by silver rays. Kara walked over to where the knights were mounted and ready.

"Farewell brave knights," she lamely recited. "May you return shining with the glory of your victory." With that, she turned and quickly walked away. Any time she was around knights, they would always try to woo her. "Probably to get to the throne," Leo would say whenever she brought it up. Kara heard the drawbridge majestically open and the thunder from the horses' hooves as the knights rode across it.

Kara started walking to her room with Leo, but a guard stopped her.

"What," Kara asked when he stepped in front of her. She knew Leo was always ready to defend Kara, no matter how harmless something seemed.

"Your father has summoned you." The guard said.

Kara sighed, him summoning her was never a good thing. The guard led her back to the throne room, where her father sat on his throne, looking very tired.

"Father?" She asked when she entered. "What is it?" The king took a deep breath.

"Kara, I have made a very hard decision today. You are to be married." He said.

Kara felt the world around her spin. "What?!" She almost shouted.

"I am sicker than I originally thought," the king explained. Between and around coughs he carried on, "and I cannot bear the thought of you carrying the weight of the entire kingdom by yourself when I pass, especially since you are so young. I want to see that you are taken care of before I die." Kara felt tears come to her eyes.

"No, father, you can't be dying! You are just sick, you're not going to die! You can't!" Her voice faded as she felt helpless and no words would fill her lips. Her father shook his head.

"I have sought any and every way I could recover, and the only medicine that can help me is across the kingdom. By the time I have sent out a messenger to retrieve and bring back the medicine, I fear," he paused, coughed, and sunk deeper in his throne, "I fear it will be too late."

"But father," Kara started. "Even if you die, and you won't, I don't need some blockheaded knight or snobby suitor to help me run the kingdom. I'll be fourteen soon father," her words coming faster and faster as though it might change his mind and halt the plan he already resolved to see through, "and I've been learning how to run a kingdom since I could understand words! Please Father. I'm not going to marry!" The king stood swiftly, a fury in his eyes.

"I am doing this for your own good, I cannot bear to have you carry a burden, that was supposed to be mine, on your own! You *will* marry, and if you do not choose a suitor, *I will*! Leo, escort my daughter to her chambers." Kara opened her mouth to protest further, but Leo put a hand on her shoulder, instantly clearing her nerves, fears, and heart. Kara turned to him, so much hurt and anger in her eyes, then strengthened her will and shrugged him off. She stormed out of the room with all the passion she could muster.

Leo quickly caught up to her as she walked like a tempest to her room.

"He has no right to do this, it's not fair! I can run the kingdom ten times better than any blockheaded man." She ranted. "What do you think?" She said, still angry.

"I believe your father does have a right, and I'm sorry, but I believe it would be best." Kara turned to him again, shoving him in the chest, even though he didn't move an inch.

"You're with them? I can't believe you!" She ran the rest of the way to her room, slamming and locking the door as soon as she was there. Then, she laid face down on her bed and cried. She knew she didn't look very royal, snorting and sniffing with her red face and puffy eyes, but she didn't care. She vaguely heard someone knock, and chose not to answer. Never before had she locked her door without saying goodnight to Leo. A part of her felt a hint of guilt for being so cold, but her sorrow screamed louder than her guilt.

After many hours, her tears were spent and the moon was out. Kara walked over to her desk. Her dragon history book sat open. She settled down and read the page it was on. In great detail, the book described where the dragons were sent. Then, Kara made a decision.

She grabbed a bag and packed extra riding clothes and the book. She placed a plain, brown cloak over the riding clothes she wore and pulled the hood up. Holding her breath she silently hoped that Leo was the earlier knock at the door. With everything in her she hoped her shadow had assumed she was resting for the night. Even Leo slept, although she wasn't sure when. Cautiously and stilling every muscle, she unlocked and opened the heavy wooden door. She saw servants slowly finishing up their day but no sign of Leo. With one last breath of relief and a quick breath in to strengthen her resolve, she snuck out of her room to the kitchen. She appeared as an errand servant with her bent back and a bag of what looked like laundry. Keeping her head down, she hoped no one saw her eyes; everything would be for nothing if she was discovered. She slipped into the busy kitchen, stole a few loaves of bread and apples, and a flask for water, then went to the stables. As silently as possible, she saddled Obsidian and put her sack in his saddle bag. Once she was done, she slowly walked the horse to the wall seemingly holding her breath with every step.

Kara looked back in the dark, the stables close enough she could still smell the hay and horses. Again, she randomly pushed against places in the wall, searching until she found the spot that moved, just an inch. Confirming that she had the right place, she pushed harder, feeling it swing out into the night air. A rush of excitement filled her as she breathed in deeply and exhaled freely, feeling a bit of relief and a bit of the unknown creeping upon her. Kara walked Obsidian out into the night, and pushed the wall closed. Mounting Obsidian in the dark wasn't difficult, and as soon as she was on him, she pulled the cloak tighter around her. She took another deep breath, turned her horse away from the wall, and galloped to the knight training grounds to retrieve a sword.

She leaned in close to Obsidian as he rode.

"Sorry father," she whispered into his mane.

"Kara?" The king knocked on her door again. "Please Kara we need to…" He grabbed the door handle and was surprised to find it unlocked. He opened the door and walked in.

"Please, come out, you must be starving. You missed lunch and dinner yesterday, come join me for dinner. Kara?" The king searched, but found nothing. Then, he saw a folded up piece of paper on her desk.

Father, I am truly sorry, but I did not learn how to rule a

kingdom every day of my life just so I can hand it all to
some stranger.
Perhaps someday I will return to the throne,
but I'm sorry, I cannot bear to be at the castle now.
I love you.

The king processed it for a minute, then sat in the chair by the desk. Tears started to fill his sleep deprived eyes, and he let his worn body bend over the letter.

With heaving breaths he sighed, "Forgive me Ella, I have lost our only daughter. Our only Kara."

Come on Obsidian, don't stop, we're almost there." They had been on their way to the Dragon Lands for three days, stopping only for short water and grazing breaks before Kara spurred Obsidian back into a gallop. They were making great time, but Obsidian was growing tired. Kara had been enjoying every moment of her newfound freedom, but as they neared the Dragon Lands, she started to have doubts.

As their journey began, they had been riding in a beautiful, green countryside; now as they drew nearer to the Dragon Lands, the ground became harsher and seemed completely devoid of life, there were less animals and far less vegetation. It was almost as if it was a forbidden land, even for animals or plants. Kara continued riding Obsidian at a slow canter, resting in the saddle as her body felt the effects of her long journey. As the ground became completely stone and turned to grey dust, Obsidian became jumpy and uneasy. He slowed to a walk.

"Easy boy, easy," Kara said quietly. For the first time she began to wonder if she had made a mistake. She surveyed their surroundings, looking for what could be causing Obsidian to feel on edge. Then it happened. Kara bent close to Obsidian and clamped her hands over her ears as the first deafening roar rattled her bones right to her soul. Obsidian reared, and Kara, unprepared, fell to the ground. Obsidian's front hooves hit the dark stone and he galloped away, back toward the castle.

Chapter Four

Dragon Lands

"Obsidian!" Kara screamed, reaching toward the horse who was feverishly galloping in the other direction. Before she could catch her breath, a shadow passed over her. From the sheer size of it, Kara knew it wasn't good. She turned her gaze to the sky and felt her heart leap into her throat. An enormous dragon flew overhead. He was at least thirty five feet from nose to tail, and was as black as coal. Kara screamed and in the same breath tried to stifle the terror escaping her lips. Her eyes widened in sheer horror as she realized the dragon had heard her. She stumbled to her feet and started sprinting as the dragon glided down toward her. Her eyes were focused on the ground, trying to avoid the terror in the sky. She ran as fast as she could, her heart beating so hard she felt like it would burst out of her chest. But, the dragon was faster. It swooped by her, plucking her off the rocks in its giant claw.

Kara started to struggle, but froze with fear when the dragon snorted and squeezed her.

"W-w-where are you taking me?" She asked, trying to keep her voice steady, while her body shook uncontrollably.

"Silence meat. Supper should not speak," the dragon said forcefully. His voice was intense and thick, warning her not to make things worse than they already were. Kara slumped in defeat, accepting that she was going to die.

I can't believe I'm going to be eaten less than a week after I'm on my own! Kara thought. Then, she remembered that she still had her sword. The dragon held her around her middle, but her arms were free, and the hilt of her weapon was visible. Kara seized the sword and exerted all her force on pulling it free. Her arms strained; it seemed as if it would never move.

"This is harder than King Arthur pulling the sword out of the stone," Kara mumbled before the sword finally came free. The dragon looked back at her with fury in its eyes a moment before Kara plunged the sword deep into its claw. The dragon screeched, and threw Kara toward the ground.

"Bad choice, bad choice, BAD CHOICE!" Kara screamed as she did backflips in the air. She caught glimpse of where she would land as she twirled head over heels through the air. The dark glimmering of a deep, blue lake grew closer and closer as Kara descended. "I'm dead," was the last thing she said before she crashed into the surface and was knocked out by the impact.

Slowly, Kara's body started to wake up. Her hands were the first thing that she could use and as she moved them just a fraction of an inch, she felt something beneath her. Her mind was the last thing to come back, and when it did, she realized she was soaking wet and laying on something that felt like moss and leaves. She ached all over and heard a small fire blazing by her side.

"Uh, what, but, where," then it all came rushing back to her. Her father deciding she was going to marry, running away, the dragon, and the fall. With a jolt she shot up, but immediately regretted it as her vision became fuzzy with black dots and her head spun. She saw she was in a cave for a moment, but that was all.

"Stay still," a voice counseled. It sounded like a boy, but Kara couldn't see very well. She settled back down, into her pillow, and rubbed her head with her hand, hoping the headache would go away.

Kara felt something pressed to her side and grabbed it to find it was her water flask. She slowly lifted her head just enough so she could drink from it. The cold water felt good against her dry, cracking throat, and she drank greedily from it. She let her head fall back onto the mossy leaf bed and closed her eyes against the headache. After a moment, she turned and opened her eyes to see who had spoken. She discovered a pair of large, silver, dragon eyes staring at her.

Kara went to jerk away from the creature, but a sharp spike of pain went through her body, stopping her from moving, so she examined the dragon in fear. It was large, and a deep dark blue, with long horns and a silver underbelly. She stayed there frozen in a half sitting up position, staring at the dragon with wide eyes. The dragon looked at her curiously, then spoke.

"Gold eyes," he said in awe. Kara tilted her head in confusion.

"What?"

"You have gold eyes," the dragon said as if it was the most fascinating thing in the world.

"Well, yes," Kara said, suddenly aware of her embarrassment. She started to ask another question, but she jumped as another, even bigger dragon landed at the entrance of the cave. It was a dusty brown hue and had frills surrounding its head. The first dragon jumped in front of her, shielding her from sight.

"Rahm," it said, its voice ancient and like the rigid grating of a thousand thunders. "Lusarth is on the move, we must fly."

"I will find you before the month's end Kusarn," Kara's dragon said. The bigger dragon grunted and took off. Then, the first one turned back to Kara.

"What is your name," the dragon asked. Kara felt a bit of her old fire return.

"Who are you?"

The dragon stood straighter. "I saved you, I deserve to know your name."

Kara swallowed her pride. "I'm Kara."

"Rahm," the dragon said curtly. Then, it turned to leave.

"Wait," Kara said, standing up quickly and wincing at the pain. "Where am I?"

The dragon snorted and turned around. "You're in the Dragon Lands."

Kara rolled her eyes. "I knew that, I meant where in the Dragon Lands?" Rahm looked at her like she was crazy.

"You meant to come here? Don't you know about the decree, or history? Or common sense?"

"You have no idea what *my* life is like! This was the best option for me!" Kara calmed herself, taking some deep breaths and trying to focus. "It doesn't seem *that* dangerous."

Rahm laughed, and Kara gave him a cold stare.

"What's so funny?"

"You were nearly eaten, by one of the worst dragons in history, two seconds after you crossed our borders!"

"But I wasn't!" Kara retorted. Rahm snorted again.

"I thought you would leave once you woke up. Apparently not. Tell me where you live, I'll take you there."

Kara stared, her mouth gaping.

"It's across the border, so you can't take me, even *if* I told you. Why do you care?" Oddly she wasn't afraid at all. She started to think that maybe she was so exhausted that she wasn't completely aware of the situation. But why did the dragon care?

The dragon shifted uncomfortably. "I, um, that's beside the point. Tell me where you live. You're not safe here."

"It's not beside the point, and like I said, you can't take me there. I'm here to stay."

The dragon sighed.

"Stay here," he said. Kara sensed a hint of authority, or was it concern? Without another thought, he turned and took off.

"Wait," Kara said, a moment too late. She sat back down with a sigh of frustration and relief. Relief because she was sitting down and it hurt less to sit down; and frustration because after finally getting to the Dragon Lands, she was being told what to do *by a dragon*.

Once Rahm was gone for more than five minutes, Kara decided to check out the cave. It was large; the ceiling almost 30 feet high. After looking around the inside of the cave, Kara decided to look outside. She walked to the mouth of the cave and gasped. The cave was located on the face of a sheer cliff. Kara scooted back away from the edge, she looked down and saw a layer of clouds below her. She sat there for what seemed like eternity. Waiting, and more waiting.

Without warning, Rahm burst through the sea of clouds, sending them into an uproar as he flew straight up with the white vapor rising up with the wind he created. He reached the apex of his flight, spread his wings out wide, and began to glide toward the entrance of the cave.

Kara gazed in wonder as she recognized just how big Rahm really was.

It took her a moment to realize that if she stayed where she was, she would get run over. She quickly scrambled to the back of the cave as Rahm tucked his wings in and stopped his momentum by digging his six, razor sharp talons into the stone. The cave was too small for him to stretch his wings even the slightest, and he had only about a foot between the ceiling and his horned head if he stood straight and tall.

As he stood in front of her, Kara noticed he was carrying something in one of his claws. A delicious aroma filled the air and Kara heard her stomach growl. A searing pain of hunger suddenly became apparent and Kara grabbed her stomach, willing it to stop complaining. All of a sudden her situation became very real. She was hundreds of leagues away from home, and she knew no one in this new world she had traveled to. Rahm stepped forward and placed what he had been carrying in front of her.

Kara felt her mouth water when she saw it was a skinned, fired, steaming deer. Rahm laid down and grabbed a leg and tore it off with ease. He started eating it, then stopped and looked at Kara, clearly confused. Kara smiled and grabbed a leg of her own, but with more effort. When the entire leg came off, she looked at Rahm, wondering if he would think it was too much, but he just kept eating. Not caring if the dragon thought she was a pig, Kara dug into the meat. As they ate, the day slowly came to an end, her brain started to clear again, and the only light that filled the dark cave, came from the small fire in between them.

She quickly ate her fill, leaving at least half of the leg unfinished. Kara watched as the dragon ate his portion.

"Why are you being so nice," she asked, breaking the silence. Rahm stopped eating and looked up at her, his silver eyes reflecting the firelight. "It has something to do with my eyes, doesn't it? I see you studying them." The dragon continued studying her, showing no expression.

"Yes," he admitted at last.

"Why?"

Rahm opened his mouth to speak, but closed it with a snap and turned his head abruptly to the cave entrance. Kara sat up into a kneeling position.

"What is it?" A moment later, her question was answered with a horrible screech.

Chapter Five

Wyverns

Kara felt the hair on the back of her neck stand straight up as goosebumps covered her arms. Rahm stood and walked to the entrance, his snout wrinkled into a snarl.

"Stay in the back of the cave," he said a moment before leaping off the edge and spreading his wings in flight. She could tell he had no desire to debate the statement, but she went ahead anyway.

"Rahm," Kara shouted, trying to stop him. "I swear if he does that one more time I'm going…" Completely ignoring his words, she watched as he flew out above the clouds, searching below him and making a downward thrust of his powerful wings every so often to soar higher. It was silence, and Kara could barely make out his dark blue form against the dark night sky. Kara almost screamed as something small burst like lightning out from below him and rammed his stomach. Rahm arched up and swooped low as the creature ascended higher. As the intruder flapped its leathery wings, Kara saw it was a wyvern. It was a rusty red color, and had curled horns like a ram. Even from a distance Kara could see its long sharp claws and the way it glared at Rahm as he circled down below it. Luckily, it was much smaller than Rahm, but the wyvern was still bigger than Kara.

It gave another piercing screech and a second wyvern shot out and attacked Rahm from below. As Rahm clawed and snapped at the wyvern trying to ram him from below, the first wyvern swooped down and dug its claws into Rahm's side, making him roar in pain. The two wyverns attacked him from above and below, tearing into him with their teeth and claws, and ramming him with their horns. As if it wasn't enough, a third screech echoed, and yet another beast rose from the night and joined the first two in tearing Rahm to shreds.

"Rahm," Kara screamed, unable to contain herself, but instantly regretting her outburst. One of the wyverns obviously heard her as its head jerked in her direction. It snapped at Rahm one last time before abandoning him to head toward Kara. Her heart jumped in her throat as the monster sped toward her, baring its shark like teeth in some kind of sick smile.

"Kara!" Rahm shouted.

Kara knew there was no escape, and there was no way Rahm was coming to her rescue. She rushed to the back of the cave where there was nothing except the half eaten deer, the fire, her flask, and her moss bed. The fire nearly went out as a strong, cold gust of wind blew in from outside. Kara turned to see the wyvern hovering in place right in front of the entrance, its wings too big for it to land while flying. It flew close to the entrance, hooking one of its long claws on the ground. It quickly folded its wings and pulled itself in and landed inside the cave. It used claws that were on its wings as its front legs as it crawled forward, hissing and drooling. Its eyes grew larger and larger as its foul breath filled the cave.

Kara desperately reached for a log in the fire as her weapon. The log seemed no better than twigs for kindling against the ravenous beast. She looked at the wyvern and their eyes locked for just a moment. Kara screamed as the beast lunged forward with unbelievable speed, ready to kill. She scrambled and fell back as the wyvern jumped to attack her. At the last moment, she held the flaming end of the log up toward the wyvern's chest, thrusting it forward, keeping her eyes locked on his jagged jaws. The wyvern stopped a very small inch from killing her, its grin turned into a snarl, and then it fell on top of Kara, dead.

Kara felt the wind knocked out of her as it collapsed. She didn't think the cave could get any darker, but somehow the dark night was growing darker every second. The motionless chest of the wyvern rested on most of her body, immobilizing her. Luckily, her head was only trapped under its wing, which created a small pocket of air so she didn't suffocate, but it didn't help much. She felt the weight of the wyvern slowly crushing her and knew that it *would* eventually kill her.

Unbelievable, I kill it to avoid being killed, and it still kills me! Kara thought. She heard a distant screech followed by another as her breathing became labored.

She could feel her lungs collapsing from the weight of the dead creature. Next, she heard the great snaps of leather wings followed by the scraping of claws on stone.

"Kara?!" Rahm said, and Kara could hear the desperation in his voice.

"I'm here," she wanted to say, but she didn't have enough breath to. All she could do was wheeze and hope that in the next moment, Rahm would think to look underneath the dead wyvern. Kara felt the wyvern move as if it was being nudged and cursed herself for not being smarter or stronger.

"Kara!" Rahm said, as if realizing where she was. He quickly shoved the wyvern's body aside and Kara gasped and coughed as she found she could breathe again. She looked up at Rahm, his face was full of concern. She could see he was covered from nose to tail in cuts and deep wounds. His breathing seemed labored as he tried to stand tall and hide any sign of pain or weakness. His shining dark blue scales were covered in green and red blood.

Kara quickly regained herself and stood to inspect his wounds, keeping in mind her bruised ribs, and still feeling the effects of the day before. Most of his cuts were wide and deep, and bleeding excessively. She could tell Rahm was tired and the way he seemed to be carrying the weight of the world, his head was down and he continued to breathe heavily.

"Lie down," She ordered. Rahm did not argue and laid his head on the ground. Kara found an especially deep wound at the base of his right shoulder. With no other options in sight, she took off her simple skirt and started tearing it into pieces. She still had on her leather riding pants on under it, thank goodness. As she tore the skirt for bandages, she found it was already covered in green blood . *Wyverns blood must be green,* she thought, shivering at the mental mention of the wyvern. After she tore up the skirt, she tied the pieces together to craft a bandage long enough to cover the wound.

"Please, be still," she counseled as she stretched the cloth over his wound. She wrapped it around him and it was just long enough for her to secure it.

"Are you alright," he asked weakly.

"Am *I* alright? *I'm* fine, it's you that you should be worried about!"

Rahm laughed, breathing out heavily as he let his body rest. "I'll be fine, as long as you can keep it from bleeding too much." There were far too many cuts to count, hundreds still bleeding all over Rahm. Kara considered herself pretty resilient and able to compose herself in many stressful situations, after all, she trained her whole life to rule a kingdom. But the sight of all the blood and being trapped in a cave with nothing but the clothes on her back; the thought of Rahm helplessly bleeding on the cold ground of the cave, Kara started to panic.

Then, she had an idea. First, she went over to her bed and wrapped handfuls of moss around her hands. Then, she steeled herself, and walked over to the dead body of the wyvern. She kicked it once, just to make sure it was dead, then bent down by its head. Its mouth was slightly agape, as if it was in mid-screech. Kara shivered as she stretched out her hand and grabbed one of its jagged teeth with her makeshift mossy gloves and pulled. Its mouth looked like a shark's, with rows and rows of teeth lined up just waiting to kill something.

A rancid stench came from it, so Kara held her breath as she pulled harder. Shivers filled her whole body as she fell backwards. She didn't even realize her success until the tooth popped right into her lap. She gagged and resisted the urge to throw up as she saw the foot long tooth was covered in wet and dried blood.

She swallowed a few times to keep herself from retching, breathing in and out between each swallow. Then, she picked up the tooth and moved to the wyvern's wing. She took another breath, then started shredding a wing with the tooth. Kara cut it until there were plenty of long strips of the leathery wing. With relief, she dropped the tooth and quickly moved back to Rahm. His eyes were closed in sleep, and smoke floated in a steady stream from his nostrils. Just the sight of steady breathing helped her breathing relax and she felt her shoulders relax a bit.

Kara quickly went to work, wrapping the strips of makeshift bandages around Rahm's many cuts and wounds. Once she had most of the bleeding cuts wrapped, she sat back and took a breath. She was covered in green and red blood, but she didn't care. She was too worried and still feeling completely mortified as the events continued to play in her mind and pulse through her veins.

For the first time in her life, she had been in real danger. Completely drained from every little bit of her day, she let herself fall flat on the ground as her breathing turned into a laugh riddled with disbelief. She smirked and almost laughed.

"Told you I could handle myself," she said to her father, even though he was nowhere near her. Her experience got her thinking. The only reason she had survived the wyvern, was because she made a weapon for herself. Kara looked around, determined not to be weaponless the next time something happened.

There was still nothing except for what was originally in the cave and the dead wyvern. She inhaled slowly as she knew where she was going to get her weapon. Kara went back to the wyvern's tooth and wings. She used the tooth to cut out a small bone from the wings and once again resisted the strong urge to lose her dinner, and closed her eyes, as she pulled the bone slowly from the wing. She went back over to her bed and braided some moss and leaves together to create something like a rope. After that, she tied the tooth to the bone using her rope. With tired eyes she looked at the finished product.

It was a weak excuse for a knife, but since it was stable and could obviously cut, Kara didn't care. By the time she was finished, the sun had begun to rise over the clouds. She heard Rahm groan and rushed to his side. Rahm slowly opened his eyes, then smiled.

"Take off the bandages," he said, sounding stronger than before. Still, Kara shook her head.

"Not a chance. Those bandages are the only thing keeping you from bleeding to death."

"You'd be surprised," he said. Without another thought, he stood and ripped off most of the bandages. Kara gasped as he revealed smooth, blue scales. She went over and touched his shoulder where there should have been a scar, but it was like nothing had happened. "I told you dragons heal fast." She looked up at Rahm, whose face had quickly gone from triumphant to sad.

"What is it," she asked.

His voice was grim. "You can't stay here."

Kara frowned, then stared sternly at him and put her hands on her hips. "Why not?"

"Really?" Rahm asked, gesturing to the wyvern with a claw. "You almost died!"

"But I didn't," she retorted. Rahm sighed.

"You're obviously mad, so I'll make a deal with you. It's apparent it's too dangerous for you to stay here," Kara opened her mouth to argue, but Rahm raised a talon, silencing her, "but it's not too dangerous for you to visit."

Kara smiled at the idea, but then frowned. "I can't. I live at the palace, and I can't go missing for a week unnoticed!"

Rahm smiled. "What if I told you I could make it so you could come and go in a day."

"How?"

Rahm smiled. "First, sleep, you've been up all night."

Kara hadn't realized it until Rahm mentioned it, but she suddenly felt like she was about to drop right where she stood. She smiled, embarrassed as a yawn escaped her tired body, then walked over to her bed and laid down. Almost instantly, she fell asleep.

Chapter Six

Home

Kara dreamt about a war. She stood on a rock outcropping while grey clouds flashed lightning overhead. She jumped as she heard a great roar behind her, louder than any thunder. She turned to see a massive, gleaming white dragon in armour that covered him from the tips of his wings to the end of his muzzle. Another roar father away made Kara turn again. There was the black dragon from her first day in the Dragon Lands, but this time he was also wearing armour and he looked more powerful than before. Kara stood motionless between the two, seemingly unnoticed.

Hundreds of wyverns and other dragons stood behind the black beast, each of them screeching and roaring, filling the air with sounds of chaos and war.

"Brother," the white dragon said, his voice rich and strong as it rang out over the distance between the two armies. "This has gone on too long, too many have fallen."

The dragon standing across from him growled. "You are weak, you do not *deserve* to be king!"

"That may be, but I cannot allow you to rule, and I cannot allow another one of my subjects to die by your claws. Duel me!"

The black dragon snarled. "Foolish brother!"

He leapt into the air, using his wings to help close the distance between himself and the white dragon. Kara screamed as the black dragon drew nearer to killing her.

She woke up with a start, gasping as she sat up quickly. Rahm stood in front of her, a concerned look on his face.

"Are you ok?"

Kara took a deep breath, shook off the effects of her dream, stood up and smiled. "Never better." Even she could tell she was unconvincing.

Rahm didn't seem to believe her, but he brushed it off. "It's time for you to go, let me show you how." Rahm stepped aside to reveal a great griffin the size of a horse standing by the entrance. It stamped and snorted, as if it was impatient.

"You have griffins!" Kara exclaimed, walking around the beautiful creature. Rahm walked up to her.

"It can fly you to the castle in less than a day and it's not likely to be spotted." Kara hugged Rahm around his neck, as best she could, unable to hold back anymore. Rahm stood there, unsure of what to do until she released him.

"But how will it know when I want to come back?"

Rahm felt relief that he knew what to do in this situation. "I've created this," He said, opening his claw to reveal a gold gem. It was almost see through and sculpted into a perfect oval. It was only the size of Kara's palm, so it looked tiny in Rahm's talon. Kara carefully picked it up to examine it. "Rub it and think of me. Then, we will be able to communicate and I will send a griffin for you. We will always meet here, but you must not be seen. Most dragons are kind, and won't attack humans, but they don't like humans in their lands. At worst, they'll make you turn back without the griffin, but still..." Kara nodded, so happy she couldn't even speak. Instead, she just hugged him one more time for a moment.

"Thank you," she said before letting go and climbing on the griffin. There was a space between the griffin's wings and its neck that kept Kara secured. "Goodbye," she said, waving as the griffin leapt off the entrance and into the sky. Kara leaned forward, clinging to the large feathers on the griffin's neck as it soared through the sky.

The griffin tucked its wings into a dive and broke through the cloud to reveal a dense, green forest below them. Kara laughed and squeezed her eyes shut as they watered from the wind. High above the trees, the griffin opened its wings and flew toward the horizon at breathtaking speed. Kara watched as the world became a blur, the griffin flew faster and faster, sometimes letting out a noise that sounded like an eagle's screech and a lion's roar combined.

It wasn't long until Kara saw the grey wasteland that she originally saw when she first came to the Dragon Lands. Kara leaned closer to the griffin and kept her eyes to the sky. No dragons were visible. The griffin continued to fly, but once human settlements became more commonplace, it flew above the cloud line. Kara watched as day turned to night. She loved seeing the sunset from this point of view. She breathed deeply and relished the emotion of freedom she was feeling.

All too soon it ended, as the griffin once again went into an eye watering dive. A moment before it hit the ground, it leveled out and landed. Kara struggled to stay on the griffin as it went through the maneuver, feeling like she would fall off at any second before it landed. She blinked a few times and quickly saw they were by the stables and the horses were going crazy.

"Who's there?" Someone shouted. Kara could see a lantern glow coming around the stables.

"Go, GO!" She whisper shouted to the griffin. It didn't need any more prodding. Instantly its wings opened and with one powerful down-stroke, the griffin lifted to the dark sky. Kara watched it ascend to the clouds, then felt a rough hand settle on her shoulder. Someone spun her around to face them, and Kara found herself face to face with a very large man with an unruly beard and bushy eyebrows that made it almost impossible to see his eyes.

"Stealing from the king's stables, eh? Oh, you're in loads of trouble missy." His voice was thick with an accent from a foreign land.

"But I'm-"

"Save it for the king," the man said, grabbing and squeezing her upper arm. He held a lantern to light the way inside the castle, mumbling to himself about not getting enough sleep. As they passed the few servants that roamed the halls of the castle on the way to the throne room, no one gave them a second glance. He quickly made his way to the king's throne room and burst in like he owned the place. His long strides carried them both as he stopped right in front of the king's throne and threw Kara down.

"Your Highness, this little rat was stealing from your stables. What shall I do with her," he asked. Kara looked up at the king and felt her heart break. Instead of the strong, happy man who once was her father, now an old, weary man with sad eyes and what seemed like a permanent frown sat on the face of the man on the throne. Kara felt tears welling up in her eyes but quickly wiped them away.

At first he barely paid her a glance before returning his weary gaze to the man. Then, he quickly looked back to Kara, eyes wide.

"Kara?" He whispered. Kara smiled.

"Hello father," she said quietly. The king smiled so widely, Kara thought his face was going to split in half. He stood and ran down the steps of the dais, to where she sat, and threw his arms around her. Kara smiled as she let him hug her, then he pushed back.

"Are you alright? You look tired? What are you covered in? You're bleeding," he continued to worry over her until she sighed and interrupted him.

"Father, I'm fine."

Her father relaxed.

"B-b-b-but, how, I..." the man behind her blabbed. The king's attention snapped to him. He stood, looking furious.

"How dare you throw my daughter on the ground as if she was a common thief." The man continued to blab until Kara stepped in.

"Father, since you never let me out of the castle, how could he have known who I was!"

The king fell silent, looking once again old and weary. "Kara, please follow me." He walked out of the throne room with Kara close behind him. He led Kara to her room, and she felt incredibly guilty when she entered. Leo was leaning on a spear by her bed, clearly tired as he looked up with dark circles under his eyes. His eyes widened and he rushed forward to meet her. Only a foot away from her, he stopped and bowed. Not wanting to have to face him after what she had done, she turned instead to her father.

"What is it?"

The king sat down on her bed with a sigh. "When you left, my heart was broken, I thought I had lost you forever, and bad thing after bad thing followed in your absence. The day after you left, a wounded and mortified knight by the name of Rogo returned from the group who traveled to kill the bull. It appears the messenger was not exaggerating when he described the fearsome bull. It killed four knights, and the fifth died later that evening from his injuries. Knight after knight has died at the hooves or horns of that bull. In all, we have lost ten knights, thirteen squires, and three errand boys to the beast. That's not even counting the countless farms and lives of innocent villagers the bull has destroyed. To make things worse, the bull seems to be growing more powerful and is heading this way." The king looked up at his daughter.

"Perhaps, now that you are home, our luck shall change." The king sighed again. "I must get back to my duties, get some rest Kara, I shall check on you in the morning." With that, he stood and left, leaving Kara and Leo alone. Kara turned to Leo.

"I'm so sorry, I was being rash, but I couldn't, I just couldn't…" She let the sentence hang. Leo nodded and put a hand on her shoulder, an expression of weary sympathy on his face.

"I forgive you, now get some rest." He too, left the room. Kara went to her bed, but she didn't sleep. She took out the gem that Rahm had given her and rubbed it. It started to glow softly.

"Trying it so soon?" Rahm's teasing voice emitted from the gem.

"Rahm, I have a problem." She said, feeling as weary as her father.

"What's wrong," Rahm asked, all joking gone.

"There's an enchanted bull laying waste to the countryside. We've lost many trained knights to it, and many many others, and it is heading toward the castle."

"Should I send a griffin to get you?"

Kara rubbed her eyes. "Not yet, but if the situation comes to it, I might have to ask you to send one for me and my father. Do I ask too much?"

"Keep in touch," Rahm said.

"I will." The stone stopped glowing in Kara's hand. She looked at it, an idea forming in her head. She went to her drawer, where she had picked up multiple miscellaneous items over the years, and chose a wire and a thin silver chain. She sat at her desk and went to work. First, she sculpted the wire around the gem to form a sort of cage to hold it in place. Then, she threaded the chain through to make a necklace.

She smiled at her work of art, blew out all but one candle, changed into her nightgown, and finally slipped the necklace on over her head before getting in bed and blowing out the last bit of light.

"Are you crazy!" Cole shouted. The warlock stood patiently. "A bunch of knights have died trying to kill that thing, and I'm just a farm boy, I'll be crushed!" The warlock shook his head.

"No, you are Cole the knight, the knight who will save this land and deliver much needed medicine to the king to win his favor. Don't forget, you have me."

Cole looked out over the field where the raving bull was stomping and bucking and bellowing fiercely. He shook his head one last time, wondering why he was listening to the strange man in front of him, then set off across the field. When he was thirty feet away, the bull noticed him, and charged. Cole felt his blood freeze in his veins as he watched the distance between them lessen until it was nothing.

Somehow, as the bull was about to run him through, he jumped and rolled to the left, dodging the bull. Without a moment's thought, he ran after the bull, jumped, and grabbed onto it, pulling himself up. Once he was on top of the bull, he lifted his sword and drove it into its back, killing it. The bull fell to the ground, eventually skidding to a stop, and Cole jumped down. Immediately the thought entered his mind, *What just happened?* There was a thunderous cheer as people who had been in hiding came out to congratulate their new hero. The warlock got to him first.

"Whistle," he hissed in Cole's ear. Cole was confused, but nonetheless, he whistled. A loud whinny answered him. A huge, white warhorse decorated in shining silver armour, to match Cole's, came galloping toward him. It stopped in front of him and reared, then settled, ready for him to mount. The warlock grabbed Cole's arm, digging his long, gnarled fingernails into it.

"Go straight to the castle, proclaim that you have slayed the bull and offer the king this," he said, pushing a small pouch into Cole's hand. "Go!" The warlock shoved Cole and hiding his disbelief he mounted the beautiful horse. He grabbed the reins and squeezed the horse's side with his legs, making the horse sprint forward into a gallop.

At full sprint, the horse made it to the drawbridge by high noon. The gatekeepers looked down at him from the tall wall.

"Who goes there," they shouted down.

"Cole the Silver, killer of the white bull!" Cole said, trying to come off as impressive. The gatekeepers exchanged a look, then shouted down the other side of the wall.

"Lower the bridge." The drawbridge lowered and Cole urged his horse to gallop across. He dismounted and handed the reins to a stable boy. Then he turned to someone who looked official.

"I wish to have audience with the king." The man looked him up and down, then motioned for Cole to follow him. The man led him into the castle, and Cole couldn't help but gawk at the interior. All the halls were well lit with windows and torches, and the walls were well decorated. A red and gold carpet lined the middle of all the floors. Cole was so busy admiring the castle, he almost ran into his guide when he stopped.

"Show respect," the man counseled, almost exasperated, as he opened a massive door. Cole looked in with wide eyes to see the king's throne room. The king was sitting on a huge throne of pure gold, seated on a smaller gold and silver throne was the princess. Cole had to admit, the princess didn't look too pretty, more average, but he saw her small silver crown and knew she was a great prize.

The king was talking urgently to a knight, but looked up as Cole strode forward and bowed in front of him.

"Who are you," the king asked, his face stern. The princess raised an eyebrow.

"I am Cole the Silver, slayer of the bull, and I have come to present myself, and offer my services and a gift to the king." He bowed and held out the small pouch. A man standing by the king's throne went and retrieved the bag, then went back to the king's side and opened it. He gasped and whispered in the king's ear.

"You bring me medicine?" The king asked. Cole gulped and hoped the warlock knew what he was doing.

"Yes, sire."

The king smiled. "You have found favor with me boy, will you stay at my palace to rest, you must be weary."

Cole returned the smile. "I would be honored to."

"Kara, why don't you show him to one of the guest rooms?"

Kara gave her father a quick, angry look, then masking her emotion, rose from her throne and walked to Cole, who tried to smile his most charming smile.

"Follow me," she said, her tone flat and expressionless. Leo followed Cole as he followed Kara. Once they were a ways away from the throne room, Cole sped up to walk by Kara.

"Who is he," he asked, concerned that the man following her was her betrothed.

"He is Leo, my personal guard. He goes with me everywhere."

Cole smiled. "I see, do you want me to get rid of him?"

Kara stopped and turned to Cole, a fire in her eyes. "To be honest, I would rather it be the other way around." She turned and continued walking, cold and hard as she all but left Cole behind. Cole felt as if everything were going wrong.

"Forgive me, I thought you weren't betrothed." Cole said. Kara sighed and turned sharply back to Leo, ignoring Cole altogether.

"Leo, would you please take Cole to his quarters? I feel I have better places to be."

Leo nodded. "As you wish, Princess."

Kara walked straight to her room, and after locking the door, she sat on her bed and grabbed her necklace. She rubbed it until it started to glow.

"What is it, are you in danger?" Rahm asked.

"No, the bull is dead."

"How?"

"A new knight came out of nowhere and killed it, he has come to the castle and given my father medicine he needed."

"Your father was sick?"

"He was supposed to be dead within a month, and no one else knew that he was sick except for me and a few of his close friends."

Rahm was silent a moment. "Keep your eye on him, I don't like it."

"Neither do I, but I have a question. When can I come back?"

"After your last disappearance, I'm sure your family will be watching you closely, as will the new arrival. Wait for things to calm down, then contact me again." A loud banging on the door made Kara turn.

"I have to go."

Chapter Seven

Trouble Rising

Kara waited for a week, going throughout her classes and trying to go without incident so she could once again be unnoticed. The king continued to pair her and Cole together for 'activities' such as archery, chess, and horse rides. Though they were things Kara usually enjoyed, being forced to do them with Cole was unbearable. Kara was convinced that her father was planning on marrying them, but she could tell he still wasn't sure.

Still, he placed Cole as Kara's second, personal knight. In secret, Kara spoke to Leo about her resentment for Cole, and Leo agreed. One day, as Kara and her father sat in the throne room, Kara's guards standing on either side of her throne, a boy came in, burned, sweaty, and mortified.

"Your Majesty!" He said, trying to bow, but falling in the process. Unable to restrain herself, Kara raced forward and bent by the battered boy. She helped him back up and looked in horror at the monstrous burns that covered his body. He still smelled of ash and smoke, and burned flesh. Before she could do anything else, Cole stepped forward and gently escorted her back to her throne. She glared at him, then turned to an errand boy standing by the wall.

"You," she said, "get him some water!" The errand boy ran out of the room as the injured boy breathed heavily.

"Thank you, princess," escaped his lips in faint whispers.

She smiled at him, and he turned to the king. Doing his best to speak in a manner fitting to address the king.

"Your Majesty, there are dragons destroying provinces to the South!" Kara felt like she had been struck by lightning.

"Are you sure," her father asked, leaning forward in his throne.

Boldly the young boy replied, "Your Highness, forgive me, but how dare you. My family has been killed by the beasts, I have had a burning house fall on top of me, and I have come face to face with one of the beasts, I stand here before you with all respect, my flesh falling from my bones, and yet you doubt me." Kara felt the world spin around her, nothing made sense. The Dragon Lands were to the North. Rahm had said most dragons were kind and were not very fond of humans in their land. Still, she looked at the burns on the boy's arms and legs, the combination of it all gave her an overwhelming feeling that she might throw up.

"Father, may I be excused." The king must have seen it in Kara's face; he nodded and waved her out. Kara, as if in a daze, walked out of the throne room. Once they were out, she nearly fell. Not as though she fainted, but she felt like her limbs had decided to stop working. Luckily, Leo was there and caught her. He put an arm around her waist and put her arm around his shoulder. He had to bend so her feet could touch the ground, but he held onto her.

When Cole tried to do the same on her other side, Leo glared at him until he backed off. Together, the three of them walked to Kara's room. Once they were there, Leo turned to Cole.

"Stand guard out here."

"But I think I could be of-"

"Stand guard. Out here," Leo said again, more sternly. Cole nodded. Leo took Kara in her room and sat her down on the bed.

"Do you wish me to stay?"

Kara just shook her head. "Thank you," was all she could muster. Leo nodded and left, closing the door behind him. Kara rubbed her gem and waited. It glowed faintly, but she didn't talk.

"Kara," she heard Rahm say. After a week of going without contact, Kara would have been thrilled to hear his voice, but she was too numb.

"We're under attack," she said, still numb.

"What, where are you, are you safe?"

"The South part of the kingdom is under attack. It'll move here soon, I know it."

"I thought Acodia was at peace with all the lands around it."

"They're not humans Rahm, they're dragons." There was silence.

"Are you sure?"

"If you had seen the boy, you would have known. They're killing people for no reason Rahm, what do I do?"

Rahm was silent again.

"I do not believe they are dragons loyal to Ranith, but I do believe that they are dragons. Tell me if they get close to the castle and I will come to get you and you father." Kara nodded, even though Rahm couldn't see her.

"Ok." She went out of her room to find only Leo waiting for her. She went straight to the throne room, where her father sat on his throne listening to Cole.

"-Please your highness, before they attack us." The king began to nod, but Kara interrupted.

"You're going to kill the dragons aren't you," she said.

"Anything to keep you safe," Cole replied.

"But you would be endangering me more by doing that."

Cole looked confused, as did everyone else. She turned to the king.

"Father, I understand we have the right to defend our people, but the dragons might not. If we kill them, the others might think it as an act of war. We would be crushed. If they come to the palace, then we have every right to defend ourselves, but until then, evacuate the South countryside, and wait. Please."

Kara knew that what she was saying wasn't true, but she knew that if Cole went ahead, he would take half an army and they would all wind up dead. The king sat, contemplating, then turned to a messenger.

"Send out an evacuation decree." He turned back to Kara. "I hope your right."

Kara nodded, thinking, *"Me too."*

———————

"She hates me, and she's convinced the king to not let me attack," Cole said to the warlock. He told the gatekeepers he had needed to stretch his horse's legs and now he was speaking to the warlock under the cloak of darkness.

"Don't worry, I will take care of it, now go, before the guards suspect. The warlock ushered Cole back on his horse and back toward the palace.

"This princess is more rebellious than I thought. I must *make* the king favor Cole quickly, then, get him out of the picture."

Kara paced in her room, searching the bookshelves for any mention of dragons, but there was nothing. She tickled the spines of the many books, her eyes darting from title to title in her frantic search. Leo stood quietly in the corner of her room, watching her with concern. Cole was also there, but he was wondering how he was ever going to woo the princess when the guard wouldn't even let him get close.

"Leo," Kara said, distracted in her search, "will you look in the castle library for anything that mentions dragons?" Leo stepped forward.

"Princess, wouldn't it be better-"

"Quickly please," she said, forgetting that she had two knights. Leo bowed stiffly then turned to exit, but didn't leave until he had sent a look to Cole that basically screamed, *"Don't even get within five feet,"* he turned and quickly left in hopes he would return sooner than later. Though Cole was terrified by the knight, he saw an opportunity. Kara reached for a book on a high shelf, but could barely touch it.

Cole straightened, walked up behind her, and reached over her to retrieve the book. Kara spun around as Cole held out the book to her. She backed up for a moment, looked at the book, then raised her chin.

"That's not the one I needed." She turned back to look more, but Cole wouldn't back off, so she was pressed between the bookshelf and him. She turned back to him.

"Move back," she said slowly. Instead, he moved a bit closer.

"Move. Back. Now," she said, slowly saying each word with as much quiet power as possible.

"Princess, you are beautiful, and it pains me to see such a pretty young woman age herself with stress."

Kara felt a fire ignite, and resisted slapping the smile off his face. "Move back now, Cole."

Cole sighed. "Princess, I would face dragons for you, why do you resent me?"

Kara felt claustrophobic, pinned between Cole and the wall. "I order you to move back."

Cole smiled. "That's no way to speak to your future husband, is it?"

Kara went from furious to fearful in a moment. Cole wasn't just out for her father's favor, he was going for her.

"Cole!" A voice shouted behind him. Cole whirled to see Leo standing in the doorway, looking eager to murder him. "Get out," he said, his voice deadly. Cole silently left, though still holding his ever growing resolve to get his way. As soon as he was gone, Kara closed her eyes and let herself sink against the bookshelf, a sigh of relief escaping her lips. She felt herself trembling, and opened her eyes as she heard the door close. Leo locked the door, then turned to Kara.

"Are you alright princess? Did he hurt you?"

Kara let out a laugh that made her sound like a maniac, a mixture of her fear and anger.

"I am never making you leave without hearing you out, again!" She wrapped her arms around herself, trying to stop trembling. She had known something was off about him, but now she definitely knew she was in trouble.

"Leo, I'm going for a long ride, alone, please." As much as Kara wanted and valued the protection Leo provided, the weight of the stone around her neck reminded her how desperately she needed to communicate with Rahm. She would have to take the risk of doing this alone.

Leo frowned, his eyebrows knitting together in uncertainty, but he nodded.

"Thank you," Kara said.

Chapter Eight

The Attack

Leo followed her to the stables, and helped her saddle up Obsidian. They worked in silence, Leo sensing that it was what Kara wanted. She quickly mounted, thanked Leo one more time, then rode out through the secret exit that only she and Leo knew about. The ground flew beneath Obsidian's hooves as she rode him across the hills outside of the castle. The long blades of grass danced in the wind, changing the shades of green as the sun reflected off each blade. Kara didn't notice. Right now, she had one thing on her mind. She rode until the castle was barely the size of a pebble, just a small figure in the distance, instead of the enormous structure she knew it was. Satisfied with her distance from home, and all the while making sure Cole did not follow her trail, she tied Obsidian to a tree. She pulled on the chain around her neck, tugging the gold gemstone into view before she slipped it over her head and off her neck. The gem felt cold, but as she rubbed it and thought of Rahm, it started warming. As soon as the gold orb began to glow, Kara spoke.

"Rahm, are you there," Kara asked.

"I'm here, are you ok?"

"I'm fine, I just want to talk to you -- not like this…"

"You want me to send a griffin?"

"Yes." There was a pause.

"It's on its way."

"Thank you Rahm." The glowing stopped and Kara slipped the necklace back over her head, and leaned against the tree. She was still slightly trembling from the experience with Cole, she just knew that there was something evil about him. Or, at least, around him.

The griffin soon arrived, and Kara's first sign was Obsidian going crazy. She stood, clenching her hands into fists and telling herself that Rahm would know what to do as the griffin dove toward her. It did the same trick it had done when it was leaving her at the castle. It opened its wings at the last second, creating a gust that nearly sent Kara tumbling.

Kara didn't waste any time, she quickly got on the griffin's back and prepared to ride. As soon as she was on, the griffin took off like a bullet. They soared above the clouds until they reached the outskirts of the Dragon Lands. The griffin descended below the clouds and Kara leaned close to its neck, hoping no dragon caught a glimpse of her. They passed through without incident, and the closer they got to the place she was meeting Rahm, the safer she felt. She watched the forest pass beneath them and took a deep, cleansing breath and enjoying her view in the cloudless sky. The griffin landed at the entrance, and waited only a moment after Kara got off before jumping into the sky once more.

Kara was the only one in the cave, there was no fire, and it was very dark, especially toward the back of the cave. Kara almost crawled to feel her way to the back, but she remembered enough about the cave that she was able to stay on her feet. She looked around until she finally felt the knife she made the last time she was there. The moment she grabbed it, a large gust of wind blew into the cave. Kara stood and turned, and she could see it was a dragon, but it was lit up from behind, so she couldn't make out any details.

"Kara."

Instantly Kara relaxed as she recognized Rahm's voice. Rahm walked to the back by her, dropped what Kara (correctly) assumed was wood, and lit it so it could provide light. Rahm turned to Kara, now illuminated by the fire.

"You wanted to talk, what is it?"

Kara sighed and sat down. "Cole, the knight that killed the bull, something is wrong about him."

Rahm lay down, keeping his eyes on Kara. "What do you mean?"

"He, got close to me, and-"

Rahm snorted, and looked as furious as Leo had. "He did what?"

Kara realized he had misinterpreted what she had said. "No, I mean we were just close -- together." Even though she said it as if it wasn't bad, she shivered at the memory. "It's just, I just feel like something's off about him."

"How can you tell?"

"When we were close, I felt a sense of," she paused, staring off; trying to find the right words, "a sense of coldness emanating from him, and I felt sick. It's hard to explain. I just don't know the words."

"Have you told anyone else about this?"

"No."

Rahm nodded. He paused, "I understand, but others might not. Keep it to yourself, and try to stay away from Cole." Rahm's head snapped toward the entrance, and he looked as if he was listening. Kara stood up, thinking it was more wyverns. But Rahm stood up slowly and calmly.

"I have to go, but tell me if anything happens." He looked at Kara one more time, before regrettably jumping off the entrance into the sky. A moment later, the griffin appeared, ready to take Kara back.

Kara returned to the castle, where Leo met her as soon as she crossed the drawbridge.

"Princess, I have good news."

Kara dismounted as a stable boy rushed forward to take Obsidian. "What is it?"

"Your father sent the decree, and since the villagers have evacuated, the dragons have retreated."

Kara smiled, eager to go see her father. As she walked across the courtyard to see her father, it started to rain. She stopped, feeling as if the rain was somehow wrong. Leo, who had been grinning as he walked by her side, also stopped.

"Princess?"

Kara didn't answer, but looked up. Dark clouds poured the rain from overhead, but she realized something. There had been no sign of clouds when she had gone to see Rahm. Instantly her fears became reality.

The first dragon, a giant, gleaming red drake, dove from out of the clouds. It stopped mid dive and grabbed onto a tower, letting out a deafening roar that shook the stones. It then released a tyrant of flames onto the walls surrounding the castle. A bell signaling that the castle was under attack began to ring out across the palace. Kara watched in horror as a second, brown dragon descended onto the side of the wall opposite to the first dragon. It also rained destruction. The gatekeepers screamed for the drawbridge to be lowered, seeing how the walls on either side of it supported dragons. Leo grabbed Kara's wrist and started dragging her toward the lowering drawbridge. The, now muddy, ground grabbed at Kara's boots as her feet slapped and battled against the wet mush.

"Hurry princess," Leo shouted over the chaos. Kara looked to the sky and pulled against Leo. Everything, happening so quickly, seemed to move in slow motion around her.

"Wait Leo-" She had slowed him down to a stop when a third dragon flew over and breathed fire on the entire wall. She and Leo were just far enough away that they felt the waves of heat, and narrowly escaped the flames. Leo turned and tackled Kara to the ground as the flames behind them roared. Kara looked behind her and felt like she was going to throw up. The entire wall was on fire, including the drawbridge. People all around her were running and screaming. As she was taking in all the chaos, she realized Leo was jumping on her feet, the hem of her dress was on fire. He quickly beat it out and helped her up.

Two dragons were sitting on the two walls, relentlessly breathing fire all around them. The third flew overhead, randomly reigning chaos. Leo tried to lead Kara to the castle, but a fourth dragon dropped out of the sky and blocked them. Kara found herself face to face with a giant, brown dragon, with steaming nostrils, and razor sharp claws. Leo reacted immediately, drawing his sword to fight, but the dragon moved its head and rammed him aside.

"Leo!" Kara screamed, she went to help him, but the dragon snapped back to her. Kara froze, looking into its eyes, then saw something. Its eyes were glazed over, and it looked dazed.

"Why are you doing this?" She asked, hoping she could reason with it. Its glazed eyes seemed to clear just a bit. "Have we offended you?" The eyes grew clearer still. "Please, talk to me!" The eyes cleared all the way to reveal piercing, red eyes. The dragon looked around, confused.

"Where am-" It interrupted itself with a painful roar, and Kara screamed as she saw what had caused it. Cole stood under its wing, his sword deep in the dragon's side.

"NO!" Kara screamed. Cole rushed forward and grabbed her, stopping her from going to help the dragon, even though she knew it was dead.

"Take the princess inside where she will be safe," he instructed another knight, handing her over to him.

"No, wait, LEO!" Kara protested against the knight that was dragging her inside the castle, but he either didn't listen or didn't care. She scrambled out of his grasp at the last second and ran toward Leo. Before she could reach him, a dragon grabbed her around the waist and flew up into the sky. Taken from the battle, all Kara could do was watch as the two other dragons destroy the castle.

The dragon holding her flew far to the south, toward one of the great forests of Acodia. He flew to the dense foliage and walked into a large cavern, holding Kara above the ground. Kara squirmed in the dragon's grasp.

"Let me go! Why are you doing this?" Kara asked the dragon, hoping to reason with it like she had with the other dragon.

"Quiet," it growled, shaking her slightly. It went to the back of the cavern where there were shackles chained to the wall. It dropped Kara and growled again.

"Chain yourself." It commanded. Kara picked up the first shackle with trembling hands. She pretended to shackle her right wrist, then moved to the next one.

"Do it right, human," the dragon said fiercely. Kara squeezed her eyes closed, willing her heart to stop beating as if it was going to burst, then pressed the shackle closed with a click. She continued to do another one on her other wrist, then she moved to her ankles. The chains had a few feet of leeway, and Kara guessed that they were only there to stop her from leaving the cave. Once she had finished, the dragon seemed satisfied and walked out of the cave.

"Wait, you can't leave me here," Kara protested. The dragon turned in a flash and jumped toward her, roaring in her face. Kara fell back against the wall and covered her head with her arms. She felt her heart stop beating and found she could barely breathe. There was so much fear, she didn't even notice the dragon leave. She sat in that position for a while, not noticing the sun leaving or the cold that settled into her bones. Then, subconsciously, she rubbed the stone hanging from her neck between her fingers, seeking comfort in her dismal situation.

"Kara?" It was Rahm's voice that spoke. It was the first sound Kara had heard since the roar, and she gasped in surprise. "Kara, are you ok?" Kara couldn't hold in her fear, so she cried. Letting the tears fall on the stone as she shivered at what she thought was sudden coldness, and a very dismal future.

"Kara, what is it? Are you alright? Kara!"

Kara finally spoke through the tears. "Dragons attacked the castle, they might have killed Leo, then Cole killed one." She stared ahead at nothing, just focusing on breathing in and out, she finally finished, "I was taken." She said it in a rush of words, trying to get it out before she started crying again.

"What, are you ok?"

"Something was wrong with one of the dragons, it wasn't attacking of its own will, but the one that took me, I…" Kara began crying again, the memory of the roar, and the cold, and her hunger being all too much. The shock seemed to be taking up residence in her whole being.

"Where are you, I'll come get you."

"I'm somewhere in the Southern Great Forest, but Rahm, the dragon might still be around."

"I'll find you," Rahm said, then the stone went back to normal. Kara took a deep breath, trying to steady herself. She heard the sound of claws on stone and stood up, looking in the darkness.

"Rahm?" No answer. Kara knew instantly that it was the other dragon. She sat back down, trying to steel herself for whatever the dragon would do.

"You look cold, human," it said mockingly.

"Yes, but I feel bad for you," she said to the darkness. As scared as she was, she would not let this dragon take everything from her.

"Why is that?"

"Because everyone knows that the coldest thing is a cold heart."

The dragon roared, scaring Kara momentarily before she realized he was laughing.

"Here, human, allow me to warm you."

Kara had to put a hand over her mouth to keep herself from screaming as the dragon sent a small puff of orange fire directly at her. She started pounding on the edge of her skirt, which had caught on fire. The dragon laughed again, breathing fire in another corner of the cave, lighting a small fire away from Kara.

Kara yearned for its warmth, but made no move toward it. The dragon gave a sick smile, which reminded Kara too much of the wyvern.

"You also look hungry, human. Here." The dragon extended a claw and tossed something a few feet from Kara. Kara stood and quickly backed away as she realized it was a bundle of snakes. They hissed and began to slither toward her. She kicked a few of them away, but one bit her ankle. Then another. Kara bit her lip against the pain and continued to fend for herself but failing miserably, getting bitten until the dragon used his claw to drag most of them away.

"I'm sorry, I assumed you liked fresh meat." It breathed fire on the bundle of snakes it collected, then devoured it.

"Why are you doing this?" Kara asked. She was sitting again and rubbing her multiple snake bites, hoping they weren't poisonous.

"Because I volunteered, human. Your species are weak. No claws, no scales, no fire. I despise your weakness, and I wish to snuff out every one of them I can. Besides," he walked closer to Kara. Kara knew something was about to happen and pressed herself against the wall. The dragon continued coming closer until he was barely a foot away from her. "Human meat tastes delicious, and I like to play with my food." Kara screamed, feeling completely helpless, as the dragon raised his claw to strike, but above her scream she heard the dragon roar in pain. Her eyes grew wide as she saw him turn quickly. She let out a cry of relief when she saw Rahm there, looking fearsome as he roared at the dragon. Kara felt her hope die as she realized the dragon was bigger than Rahm.

"Hello, your highness," the dragon hissed as he turned sharply to attack Rahm. The dragon leapt forward, his talons extended as he lunged for Rahm. Rahm dodged it and breathed a stream of white hot fire at the dragon's face. The enemy dragon reared up, screaming more than roaring as it clawed at its singed face. Rahm ran around it and bolted toward Kara.

"Are you alright?"

"Behind you," Kara screamed as the dragon went to bring a claw down on Rahm. Rahm jumped aside in the nick of time, but Kara couldn't move. The claw landed a foot or so in front of her, and she shrunk back from it. The dragon turned to Rahm, who had run to the entrance again. It breathed a torrent of orange fire right at Rahm. Kara watched in fascination as she saw Rahm fly upward out of the flames, but the dragon just followed him. Rahm swooped, and twirled, and flipped in the air, avoiding the fire.

The dragon stopped for a moment, and Rahm landed on the ground. Kara could see he was wearing out. The dragon turned its head and looked back at Kara before laughing. Kara tried to move, but she was petrified as the dragon reached back and grabbed her. He yanked her away from the wall, making Kara yelp in pain as the chains momentarily cut into her hands before snapping.

"So you came to save the human," he said humorously laughing again. The dragon squeezed Kara slightly, making her double over gasping for air. When Kara looked back at Rahm, she almost didn't recognize him. He looked so fearsome, ready to kill the dragon. Surprised by her own reaction, she realized she was scared of him for a moment.

"Let, her go."

The dragon laughed at Rahm's demand.

"As you command." The dragon threw Kara up in the air screaming and opened its mouth for her to fall in. Kara saw her life flash before her eyes as she fell downward, closer and closer to death. At the last second, Rahm flew over her, grabbing her around the waist and away from the dragon as its jaws closed with a snap. It turned with a murderous expression on its face as Rahm landed at the back of the cave, gently setting Kara down.

"That princess must be dead by the time the knights come!"

"You will not touch her," Rahm said, his mouth already filling with white light.

The dragon also prepared to breath fire at Rahm. Kara barely had enough time to scramble behind Rahm before they both released scalding fire. Kara couldn't even look, the fire was too bright, but when she heard the dragon scream and roar, she knew who had won. She could sense a sudden calm about Rahm that told her it was over. She walked around Rahm to see the dragon, lying down, defeated. It was struggling to live as it uttered, "Your father cannot hold the throne forever." Those were his last dying words before going limp, dead. She didn't think it was possible to hate the beast more than she already did. Now that Kara was finally safe, her legs decided to stop working. She fell to her knees, her eyes locked on the dragon that nearly killed her. She sat there for a while, saying nothing as she looked into the dead dragon's eyes. As she sat, she tried to process all the horror that filled, what started out to be, a normal day. Then, her eyes grew wide as a question entered her mind.

"Why did he call you, 'Your Highness'?"

Rahm looked at her as if she was mad, there was no immediate response. She wondered if she had imagined it.

He opened his mouth but all that came out was a simple, "What?"

Kara stood and looked Rahm in the eye. "That dragon called you dragon prince."

"That's what you're worried about?" Rahm asked in disbelief.

"Yes," Kara answered.

"Are you alright?"

Kara glared at Rahm, her father had done this many times, but she would not let him change the subject.

"Rahm, answer me."

He shifted uncomfortably, and sighed. Opening and closing his mouth a few times, it was as though he couldn't will the words to come. Then finally in one breath of air, the words fell out like a river of water that almost knocked Kara off her feet.

"Because I am the dragon prince."

Kara felt her jaw drop. A new flood filled the cave. This time a flood of silence between the two. Kara sat and digested the words she never expected to hear.

"You're," as she tried to finish her sentence, her mind played out all kinds of scenarios about this friend she felt she knew. She always felt there was more, but quickly realized maybe the more wasn't so mysterious, they were more alike than she ever imagined, "you're, the dragon prince." She let out another sigh, with thoughts still filling her head, the only word that escaped her mouth was a simple, "Oh." Kara felt so many emotions at once, she thought she would explode.

"Why did he call you the princess?"

Now it was Kara's turn to be uncomfortable. She had always wondered if Rahm knew her station in life. She had no plans of telling him, just wanting to enjoy being normal and not revered for any other reason than kindness and friendship. And she felt that undeniably with Rahm. She realized just how naturally, quickly, and seamlessly their friendship formed. She wondered many times just how much he could see when she spoke through the stone. This answered her question.

"I guess for the same reason he called you 'Your Highness'."

This time it was Rahm's eyes that widened.

"You're the princess?!" Kara nodded. Rahm groaned. "Father is going to kill me." As puzzling as his comment was, Kara was exhausted and was grateful for the stillness in the air and the silence that surrounded them. Before long she gave into the exhaustion of all that had transpired. Her body sank heavily into the ground beneath her and she slept.

Kara woke to see Rahm staring out of the cave, she sensed a tenseness but she was not sure why. Just as she began to speak, Rahm interrupted.

"There are people coming," he said. Kara stood up and walked, past Rahm, to the entrance - with Rahm staying where he was behind her. She could see torchlight through the trees with the sun just starting to rise over the horizon.

"You should go, before you're seen." She said. Rahm looked at her, with an emotion that resembled regret. She felt it too, as he nodded and flew into the sky.

"I see her, I see the princess!" A group of guards and knights on horseback burst through the trees, hunting hounds barking around the horse's hooves.

"Princess," someone called. Kara smiled as she recognized the voice. Leo strode forward on his horse, his arm in a cast and more cuts and bruises wrapped on his body. He dismounted and rushed forward, bowing right in front of her. Kara, however, did not bother with formalities. She bent down and hugged him, almost forgetting about all the turmoil that filled the previous day. The men must have traveled all night.

"You're alive!" She said, so glad he was alright. She looked over his shoulder and saw Cole, sitting on his grand horse, looking very confused. His words quickly betrayed him and became very telling.

"Princess, how did you escape the dragon?" His shock written clearly across his face. Kara felt a lump form in her throat. She couldn't tell them about Rahm, but how could she explain the dead dragon in the cavern. Then, an idea came to her.

"It was unreal, it just happened so suddenly just as I thought my life was ending, it blew up. It went to breath fire, but in a strange twist of fate, it kept its mouth closed, so it killed itself." The knights looked at each other, and a few dared to venture inside the cavern. Kara watched Cole's face closely, the sun now offering more light. She began wondering exactly what his plans were now.

"Well, princess, you must be exhausted. Here," Cole said, extending his hand to her. Kara sighed. She knew she couldn't ride with Leo since his arm was broken. Yet she still didn't want to ride with Cole. Reluctantly, Kara accepted his hand and got on the back of his horse. Once again, the closeness brought back the cold she felt that seemed to emanate from his whole being. His voice startled her as she settled in behind him.

"To the castle!"

Chapter Nine

The Final Decision

As soon as the group got back to the castle, a flustered scribe ran up to her, stuttering and hyperventilating.

"Princess! Your father! He wishes to see you immediately!" He finally sputtered out. Kara glanced back at Leo, who shrugged. She rushed behind the scribe as she followed him through the halls in her ruined dress. Leo walked swiftly behind her, trying to keep his arm steady as they marched through the crowded hallways. The scribe led Kara to the throne room, where her father, looking sickly and tired, sat on his throne.

"Father?" Kara barely recognized him, seeing only a shell of what had once been a great man. The king looked up, and Kara saw a glimpse of happiness in his otherwise sad and tired eyes.

"So, Cole was successful in the rescue."

"Well, actually-" Kara began, but the king interrupted her.

"Kara, he is strong, and brave. He protected the castle from the attacking dragons and then saved you. The people look up to him."

Kara's eyes widened, realizing where he was going with his praise "Wait, father, are you-"

"Yes, I am getting sicker, and Acodia needs a king and queen. Kara, I have been thinking about a husband for you, and Cole appears to be the best choice." Kara opened her mouth to argue, but her father bent over and began to cough. It was a deep, chest rattling cough that wheezed out of him and seemed to steal a little more of his life with each heave of his frail frame. Kara closed her mouth and watched as his advisor helped him off his throne away to his room.

Kara walked back out of the throne room dismayed. *This can't be happening, s*he thought to herself. She continued walking toward her room, thinking back on everything that had happened. She longed to rest her tired aching body but rest would have to come later. She knew something was wrong. The dragon that had landed in the courtyard, something had been amiss with him. He hadn't been attacking of his own free will. He was under someone's power. It was as if his eyes had been trying to speak to her.

Kara felt the hairs on the back of her head stand up, as if someone were watching her. She stopped and looked down the hall behind her. She caught a glimpse of an awkward boy with jet dark brown staring at her, before he quickly looked away. Kara paused and stared a bit longer at the boy, but then she noticed Leo looking at her. She shook her head and started walking again. It didn't take long before Cole found Kara walking to her room.

"What did the king want?"

Kara took a deep breath and reminded herself that if she murdered him, her father would be displeased. "He wanted a private counsel with *me*." Her response was sharp and quick, hoping that he would realize she had no desire to converse with him.

"Why?"

Kara turned to him.

"There is a reason it's called *private*." She turned again and kept walking. Cole didn't follow, instead, he turned and walked the other way.

Once Kara was in her room, she turned to Leo, who had been silently following her.

"Well?" She wanted to know his thoughts.

Leo looked at her confused. "Well, what?"

"Well, do you agree with my father?"

Leo stayed silent a moment, then spoke in broken fragments as if trying to convince himself. "It would be beneficial for Acodia to have a king and queen... Cole appears to be the best choice...But no...There is something about him I do not trust."

Kara felt a wave of relief wash over her.

"But it doesn't matter. Your father has decided, and there is nothing I can do."

Kara felt the relief die as quickly as it came. She sighed and sat on her bed. "What am I going to do?"

There was a knock on her door and she saw Leo tense. She rolled her eyes and gave permission to enter. A maid walked in.

"Your father wishes to see you, he's in his quarters."

Kara took a deep breath and followed the maid, feeling as though this day might never end. She had never been to her father's quarters, not since her mother's passing, and she felt her gut twist at the thought that he needed her to come to there, rather than the throne room. She rushed to her father's quarters, but continued to feel as if she was being watched. Every so often she looked over her shoulder and caught the boy with brown hair staring at her, before busily doing something.

The maid led her through the hall, until they came to a sturdy oak door. The maid bowed and walked away, leaving Kara and Leo standing in front of the door. Kara lifted a hand to knock, but hesitated, scared at what she would find. She took a deep breath, closed her eyes, and knocked hard three times. The door opened and a physician stepped back to reveal a dark room. Kara stepped in and saw her father sitting in a chair with his advisor by his side. He lifted his head and acknowledged Kara.

"Kara, Cole has a guest, someone he considers very close. I am not fit to greet him, so would you?" Kara nodded and swallowed a lump in her throat. The king smiled. "They will be in the throne room, thank you." Kara nodded again and the physician led her and

Leo out of the room. Kara took a deep breath, brushed off her orange silver gown, and set off to the throne room. Once again, the cold feeling returned. Something was not right.

She and Leo were the first to enter. Kara took a seat on her throne. She looked longingly over at the empty thrones beside her, then snapped back as the doors opened again. Cole strode forward and bowed deeply.

"Princess, I present, my mentor and friend, um, well…"

Kara stared confused at him as he sputtered. Then, an old man with a gray beard and a brown cloak walked in. He stopped beside Cole and bowed.

"Your Highness, I, am Rogar."

Kara smiled, trying to be sweet, but when the man looked back up at her, there was something in his eyes. A look that told Kara he knew something awful, and it had to do with her. She felt that the enemy dragon was not the only beast trying to defeat her.

Will all the royal formality she could muster she greeted him. "It is a pleasure to meet you Rogar. Forgive my father, he is not feeling well, but he should be better soon." Rogar nodded, and Kara turned to a servant. "Please escort Rogar to a room."

"Actually, your highness," Rogar said, "I am a bit of an alchemist, and I would love to see the castle library to further my studies." Kara was wary, but nodded.

"Thank you."

The servant led Rogar away, and Kara stood. She walked past Cole out the door, and ran right into the brown haired boy.

She had seen him from a distance, but now, she realized he was tall. Really tall. He quickly looked away before Kara could get a good look at his face. He turned to walk away, but Kara grabbed his arm.

"Who are you," she demanded, surprisingly as tired as she was, the new day left her feeling stronger than she thought possible. The boy turned back, keeping his eyes down, and cleared his throat.

"I'm, Tobias." He said quickly. Kara frowned. She had heard that voice before, but she knew she had never seen the boy. She paused for a moment, trying to look at the boy's eyes, but he turned.

"Excuse me, I have, um, chores." He quickly walked away, leaving Kara staring after him. Leo placed a hand on her shoulder and gave her a concerned look.

"I'm fine," she said. "I'm going to the stables." She said the words as if she wanted to go alone, but she knew Leo would follow.

She spent the rest of the day at the stables. Riding and working Obsidian, she couldn't get her mind off of the events of the past two days. First, she had been captured by a dragon, kept in a cave against her will all night, rescued by morning light, and at the risk of thinking herself dramatic, the worst was yet to come as her father declared she was to marry Cole. Kara shook her head to try to get rid of the thoughts as she returned Obsidian to his stable that evening.

"Your Majesty-" A meek voice said behind her. She turned to see an errand boy standing behind her, his eyes to the ground as he twisted his hat in his hands. "Your father..." Kara felt fear seize her heart. She pushed past the boy and ran to the castle. As she rushed through the halls of the castle, she ignored the questioning looks, or Leo's calls for her to wait. Everything seemed muffled and her eyes blurred with oncoming tears. The day had been long enough.

She ran to her father's room, and entered without knocking. Physicians and the king's advisor were gathered around her father's bed, and she pushed through them and saw her father, laying back on pillows, breathing shallowly and grey. Kara knelt by the bedside and looked into her father's eyes. He gave a weak smile.

"Hello Kara, I wish you didn't have to see me like this." Vivid flashbacks of her mother's last moments came into Kara's mind, and she felt a tear escape and make its way down her cheek.

"You will be fourteen and a beautiful young lady in four days my dear, so I have a request. Don't have a week of mourning. Let it be three days, then celebrate your birthday."

"There will be nothing to celebrate." Kara said. Her father shook his head.

"Kara, three days of mourning."

Kara nodded, and the king sighed.

"Kara, the kingdom needs strong rulers. I believe, you and Cole will make Acodia prosper. Promise me, you will be strong, wise, and just in your ruling." Kara nodded.

"I promise."

"I love you Kara," the king said, putting a hand on Kara's cheek. Kara grabbed it, and the king smiled and closed his eyes. Kara felt his hand go limp in hers, but she didn't let go. She stayed still, staring at her father as she felt tears run down her cheeks. As Kara realized the truth, great sobs racked her body. She shook and sobbed, unable to contain herself. Silently, one by one, everyone left. After minutes of silence and stillness, Kara gently placed her father's hand by his side and willed herself to stand up. She felt a familiar hand on her shoulder and turned to face Leo. Without a word, he pulled her into a hug. Minding his injuries, they sat beside one another, and she let the weight of her crumbling world flow through her tears onto his shoulder. She wished she could remain in the sanctuary he provided forever. Leo softly placed a hand on her back and let her cry until her tears were spent. She mustered the last bit of strength that she didn't know she had and pushed back and looked into Leo's eyes. He wasn't blood related, but she felt he was the only family she had left.

"Thank you."

Leo nodded. Kara composed herself, then walked out of the room into the castle hallways. The king's advisor stood by the door and joined her as she walked dignified through the halls. She noticed the boy with brown hair staring at her, but ignored him, not caring anymore. After a moment of walking, the advisor spoke.

"The kingdom has been alerted of the king's passing, the week of mourning will begin."

"No," Kara said.

"What?"

"My father wished it to be three days, and so it will be." The advisor nodded.

"And we will be wed on the fourth." A voice said behind her. Kara turned, knowing who it was. Cole stood behind her, smiling.

"How dare you-" Kara started, but Cole raised a hand.

"I'm extremely sorry for your loss, but the king had a private meeting with me. He told me that upon his death and after the mourning, he wanted us to be wed as soon as possible." Cole grabbed Kara's hand. "Together, we shall rule." Kara lifted her chin and extracted her hand from his.

"If it was my father's wish, how can I refuse?" She said coldly. She felt ready to punch him in the face, but Leo stepped between them. He quietly led Kara to her room, where she thanked him again, then bid him goodnight. The day had been long and she hoped sleep would come easy.

Chapter Ten

Plot Revealed

The first day of mourning passed. Kara tried her best to stay composed for the crowd as her father was laid to rest alongside her mother at the family crypt.

"My father was extraordinary. He was selfless, kind, and just. He was never cruel, but reigned as a great king. There were so many great and small acts of kindness, that character was ingrained in him so deeply that there is not enough time in a day, or even a month, to say them all. I only hope, that as I lead and rule, I may be half as great as he..." She couldn't bring herself to speak the final word of her speech -- **was.** *Half as great as he* **was.** It made it all too final and reminded her that now she would only have the past with her father. There would be no future. Kara finished her speech and went back to her room, where she sat and stared out the window, hoping she would eventually be able to move on. Not just move on, but move on and feel again. Feel the freedom and joys of life that now seemed so distant and long ago.

The next day, as she was exiting the dining hall, she saw Rogar leaving his room with scrolls in his hands.

He looked around, as if making sure no one saw him, then quickly walked away. Kara turned and looked at Leo, who still followed her everywhere. He shrugged, and Kara walked to the door of Rogar's room. She found it was locked. So, she took a pin out of her hair and bent down to the lock.

She quickly unlocked it and opened it. Inside the room, there was a desk, a bed, and chairs. As her eyes continued around the room, the normal appearance of things turned to anything but that. She could sense the moment she opened the door that this room was anything but normal. There stood a large cauldron, and all the drapes and windows were closed as the cauldron glowed green. It was the only light in the room. Kara walked to the cauldron, and jumped as the door closed. She spun around to see Leo had closed the door.

She breathed a sigh of relief and turned back to the glowing cauldron. The liquid inside was swirling slowly, and Kara resisted touching it. She looked back at Leo still on edge.

"Why does Rogar have all this?" She asked.

"He is a dark warlock." A wispy voice answered. Kara whirled toward the voice but saw no one. Then the cauldron swirled more, and an image was revealed. Kara looked into the cauldron and saw a younger Rogar riding a giant black horse. They were both in armour and Rogar was casting spells, laying waste to a small village. Kara's eyes widened and she looked at Leo, who was equally surprised.

"Why is he here?" She asked slowly and uncertainly, her mind racing taking it all in. The image changed to show an image of herself.

"To restore his powers." the voice came again. Kara gulped. She felt fear creeping into her bones. She wished she were 3 years old again with both parents at her side thinking there was no evil, no bad, only happiness and peace. She shook her head and faced the reality that seemed so unreal.

"How," she asked hesitantly. The image formed into a knife.

"By killing you!" The voice came as less of a whisper this time.

"Never!" Leo said defensively. Kara stepped back from the cauldron in fear, and then heard the door close again. Leo was beside her, and they both spun around to face Rogar and Cole.

"Kill the man, we need the girl," Rogar said. He seemed so calm and collected as he gave the order, as if it were nothing. Cole raced forward, his sword high, but Leo had drawn his sword the moment the cauldron had announced Rogar's motive, and Leo rushed forward. Their swords met, the sound of steel on steel ringing in the dark room.

"Run Kara!" Leo shouted. Kara wanted to, but Leo and Cole were in the way, and Rogar stood in front of the door. There was nothing she could do, she was trapped. Cole swung low, but Leo stepped back and blocked it, before kicking forward with his leg. Cole jumped back, but Leo didn't let him recover before running at him with a series of forceful blows, all of which Cole parried and blocked. Kara watched hoping at some point Rogar might move and she might be able to escape.

"Just kill him already!" Rogar said. Cole smiled sickly. Kara watched in horror as Cole lunged forward and sliced Leo's hand, making him drop his sword. With his other hand in a cast from the dragon attack, Leo had no way to defend himself.

"Leo," she screamed. Leo looked back at her for a moment, for the first time fear showing in his eyes. He looked at Kara as if to say *I'm sorry*. And before Kara could utter another word or even process all that was happening, Cole plunged his sword into Leo. Kara let out an unearthly scream as Leo fell to the ground. She raced to his side, knowing even as she pressed her dress to his chest to stop the bleeding that he was gone. Her entire world was crumbling like old ancient stone that once was so strong. Her last support was ripped out from under her as Leo's last breath escaped his lips. She cried, fat tears rolling down her cheeks as she accepted the truth. What was left? What did anything matter? For only a moment she felt defeated, but the princess blood that was taught to be resilient for so many years began to boil inside her.

In a moment, her sadness and grief turned into rage. She screamed in anger and sprung forward toward Rogar, fury blazing around her, but Cole caught her around the waist and pinned her arms to her side.

"Let me go," She shouted, kicking and punching, trying to get free. "Help!" She screamed, hoping someone would hear her and come to her aid.

"Rogar, someone will hear her!" Cole said. Rogar stepped forward and waved a hand, instantly everything went black for Kara.

When she opened her eyes, she found herself chained to a hard, stone wall. Shackles, again. Her feet were also chained to the wall, this time she was positioned so her feet were dangling above the ground.

"Ah, you're awake." She heard Rogar say. Kara turned and squinted against torchlight. She could see she was in a cell, with locked bars and Rogar leering through them. Kara struggled against her confinements, but they were stable, and locked into place. There was no escape.

"I just wanted to let you know that everything will be taken care of. We will say because of your father's recent passing, you wished for a very private birthday and wedding. Then, we will say you disappeared, after the wedding of course, leaving Cole as king, me as his advisor, and you dead. I may not be able to kill you myself, but after your birthday, Cole will put you out of your misery and all will be well." Rogar rattled off his plan with such ease, as if he were listing off simple chores for the day. No feeling, no anger, not even resentment. He was truly evil. Kara shook with anger and fear, not knowing which emotion was more apparent. She tried kicking out with one of her feet and felt a slight bit of give on the shackle. For a moment, Kara felt a burst of hope, but it faded as she realized Rogar saw it too. He smiled.

"Looks like you still have some fire. I'll have to take care of that." Rogar uncapped a bottle, then reached through the bars toward Kara. He spread his fingers and Kara felt something tingle in the air, something evil. Kara gasped abruptly, and felt like her life was being slowly ripped from her, until he dropped his hands. Kara's vision was fuzzy, and her head spun as her body ached.

"There we go," Rogar said, satisfied. Kara shook her head, trying to clear her mind. She vaguely heard Rogar leave, and he took the torch with him, so Kara was left in complete darkness. After a while, feeling came back to her body. It ached and was still was weak. She feebly strained against her chains, but it did nothing except make them bite into her wrists and ankles.

She tried leaning forward, and felt something she had forgotten. The weight of Rahm's necklace hung from her neck. Her eyes widened with hope as she realized they must not have seen it, or they did not know its significance. Kara struggled, but couldn't reach the gem. So she hung there, helpless. The moment of Leo's death played itself over and over in her mind, and she cried. For all the years, Leo had been more of a father than the king. Kara still loved her father, and grieved his death, but Leo's death was for her, he died defending her. And now, it was in vain.

Kara jumped as she saw torchlight fill the passageway outside of her cell bars. *"No, I can't let Cole win."* She thought, but she knew there was nothing she could do about it. So she hung and watched in fear as the torchlight got closer, and closer. A moment before the light reached her cell, it stopped. Kara heard the cell door next to her open, then something being dumped on the ground. She tried calling out, but her mouth refused to open. Feeling utterly defeated, she hung, and watched as the torchlight left once again.

After what seemed like hours of silence, Kara heard a groan in the cell next to hers.

"Who's there?" She said as loudly as she could, but it was still only a whisper. Only silence answered. "Please, tell me who you are."

"Kara?" A voice said, and Kara recognized the voice.

"Tobias?"

"I'll get us out, hold on," Tobias said. She heard him walk around his cell, bang the bars, and then silence. She heard him making frustrated noises.

"Tobias, there is no way out," she said, all hope gone. Then a thought came to her. "Why are you here?" She had regained her some of her strength, but there was still nothing she could do.

The door at the end of the staircase opened, and torchlight filled the darkness. She heard guards speak, and felt a flicker of hope reignite. They stopped outside of her cell, and one got out a keychain and began lazily flipping the keys through his hand.

"Hurry, get me out of here," Kara said urgently.

"Quiet," one of the guards said gruffly. Kara stared at him in angry confusion.

"What?"

"I said quiet filth, King Cole the Silver will decide your fate soon enough." Kara felt a lump the size of a mountain gather in her throat. *King Cole,* she thought.

"But I am the Queen!" The guards laughed before opening the door. One walked off down the hall while the other entered her cell. As soon as he opened her cuffs, she kicked him hard in the chest. As he doubled over, she jumped sideway and ran. Doing her best to get her feet under her and push past the spells that seemed to consume her, Kara darted out of the cell, then she slammed the door shut behind her before bolting down the hall using the walls to strengthen her as the spells seemed to pulse in and out of her body. Unfortunately, she didn't make it farther than five feet before she ran into the second guard. He was larger than almost any man, and he grabbed her arms, and pinned them to her side. He hit her hard against the wall behind them. Her vision danced, and she heard the creak of the cell door and knew it was over.

The other guard appeared. "The King will probably just sentence her to death anyway. We would be doing him a favor getting it done down here."

Kara eyes grew wide in horror as the guard in front of her drew a sword and stepped back to deliver a fatal blow. This was it. Her vision was still blurry, but she saw the guard's face go from a wicked grin to being completely ripped with pain, before he and the sword fell forward. Tobias stood behind them, a bloody sword in his hand. She made eye contact with him, just long enough to see his eyes. His silver eyes. That was the last thing she saw before being knocked out by the guard holding her. Even as her vision went black, she thought of one word. *"Rahm."*

Rahm watched in horror, up to the point where the guard pulled his sword, then he decided it was time to act. He had met Kara's eyes for a moment after killing the guard, but the other guard holding her, brutally smashed her against the wall. Kara slumped forward when the guard released her, her hair covering her face. The guard lunged forward with his sword, sticking it through the bars. Rahm jumped back, but not too far, then jumped forward past the sword, and grabbed the man's hand. With one deft twist, he jerked the sword out.

"Thanks!" With two swords, he put a quick end to the bewildered guard. After that, he bent down and grabbed the keys off of the first. He quickly unlocked the door, and ran to Kara. The guard had probably killed her, and he quickly pushed Kara's hair out of her face, looking for any signs of life. He relaxed as he saw her chest rise and fall.

"Kara," he said quietly, shaking her shoulder. "Kara," he spoke a bit more urgently. Her breathing changed and she brought a hand to her head. She groaned but didn't open her eyes. Rahm was a bit surprised. He would have expected her to be out for much longer than the short moment, but he wasn't complaining. Kara finally opened her eyes and looked up at Rahm.

"Rahm, but, how are you here?" Kara said weakly. She was so confused, she could barely say it. Rahm looked at her, hesitated, then explained.

"I was worried about you after you were captured by the dragon, I left so quickly, I wanted to make sure you were okay."

"But, you're a dragon." Kara said, still wondering how he was human.

"Dragon royals have the ability to maintain two forms. One is human, the other is our true form." Rahm explained hastily. He helped Kara up and let her lean on him. He helped her walk out of the cell toward the exit.

"What happened," he asked.

Kara smiled. "I thought you were spying on me."

"I lost track of you," Rahm replied. Kara sighed in grief, knowing she would have to explain.

"Leo and I found out that Cole was here only to gain the crown. He was working with Rogar, a dark warlock who was at risk of losing his power. He plans on killing me to restore his powers fully." Rahm nodded, as if it made sense. Her head was still pounding and putting the words together made it feel as if it was continuously being thrown against the wall.

"Where's Leo?" Rahm asked, he knew that the bodyguard was important to her, he had seen the way she hugged him when he found her in the forest. Kara swallowed the lump in her throat.

"He died...fighting Cole."

Rahm looked at her, concerned. "Are you okay?"

With a pounding head and her world having been completely destroyed in front of her, the question seemed completely senseless. *Okay? Really?* She thought.

"My father is dead, Leo's dead, and two power hungry lunatics are out to kill me. Yes, I'm fine," she numbly joked. Rahm looked at her and smiled.

"Glad to see you still have your sense of humor." He helped her walk up the winding staircase that led to the castle.

"So, what is the plan?" Kara asked.

"I'm taking you to the Dragon Lands."

"And?"

"We'll figure something out." He said. Kara stopped.

"I can't abandon my people!"

Rahm shook his head.

"It's too dangerous for you here. The Dragon Lands is the safest place for you."

Kara knew he was right, and as they reached the top of the staircase and met a door that opened into the castle, she mentally agreed with him.

"Once we get out of the castle, I'll return to my usual form and take you to the Dragon Lands."

Chapter Eleven

Runaway

"What?" Cole shouted. The warlock nodded.

"This is how you will become king. Just follow me down, kill her, then you will reign and I will counsel you as your trusted advisor."

"But she's the queen!"

Rogar shrugged. "What did you expect? You could be held accountable for high treason after what you have done."

Cole took a deep breath. "Fine, take me to her."

Rogar smiled and led Cole down to the dungeon. There were many cells, but none were used. Since the era of peace, there had never been need for the castle dungeons to be in use. Rogar led Cole toward the very last cell, but stopped. Two cell doors were open and there were two dead bodies outside of one. When the guards he had sent down did not return, Rogar figured that they had carelessly forgotten, yet there were their bodies.

"Where is she?" Cole asked. Rogar felt a surge of anger, followed by calm.

"Perfect, this is even better." Rogar said.

"How?" Cole asked.

"There was a dragon here, in human form. That means he was a royal. I can sense his magic was here. We can claim that dragons stole the princess, then say they killed her." Cole just stared.

"But, then how will *we* kill her?"

"We go to war." Rogar said it as if it were obvious, all these questions were irritating and the answers seemed so obvious to Rogar. Cole was becoming a nuisance.

"Are you mad! Half the kingdom would die, if not all of it!"

Rogar shook his head. "I have an ally."

"What do we do now?" Kara asked. She was standing at the edge of the cave entrance, looking out over the sea of clouds. In such a short time, this place had become like a second home to her, and now it was the only place she was safe. The daylight was just breaking but Kara felt as though she had been up for weeks.

"We have to wait." Rahm replied.

"I can't just let Cole rule the kingdom. Though, he won't rule as much as he will be a puppet for Rogar." Kara sighed and leaned against the cave wall closing her eyes. Rahm looked at her, uncertain. He wanted to help her, but he knew even seeing her was breaking all his father's laws, so there was nothing he could do.

"My father's dead. My friend is dead. Dead at the hands of a deranged man, not even a man, a boy! A deranged boy wanting the throne. A boy who is backed up by an evil warlock out to kill me." To hear herself say it outloud seemed unreal. She sighed, fighting anger, tears, and exhaustion. "And to top it all, I'm spending my fourteenth birthday in what used to be the most dangerous, but is now the safest, place for me! When exactly did my life become a horrible nightmare?" Rahm wanted to comfort her, but he turned his head out to look over the sea of clouds.

Kara noticed. "What is it?"

Rahm sighed and looked at her. "I have to go, I'm sorry. I'll be back."

Kara nodded, staying silent as she stared at the sky. She was getting used to these sudden departures. All she craved was one day of peace. Something told her that was not going to happen today.

Rahm jumped out of the cave and spread his wings, flying farther and farther away. It wasn't long until he couldn't see the cave anymore. He flew quickly over rocky terrain and past giant pillars of stacked rocks, signs that he was getting closer to his father's domain. A roar from his right caught his attention. He turned his head to see a large dragon fall into flight next to him, then another. More dragons joined him as he got closer to the great mountain. Rahm pumped his wings to fly higher and higher, trying to reach the top of the mountain where his father was waiting.

As soon as he passed the clouds, the mountain dipped into a huge crater. It sloped inward, steps carved into it. The size looked as if the steps were made for giants. Hundreds of dragons flew down and landed on the steps, which served as seats and ledges for them. Rahm flew to the bottom, where it leveled out into a giant platform. He sat alone in the bottom of the crater, and he scooted back into a shadow and listened attentively to the dragons above him as they conversed. A majority were wondering why so many of them had been summoned by Rahm's father.

A great roar that shook the mountain silenced everyone, and a giant shadow passed over the gathering. All the dragons bowed as a white dragon flew down to Rahm and landed; spreading its wings wide before elegantly tucking them to its side. The dragon was at least thirty feet long, and had a head crowned with gleaming horns. A smaller, rusty brown dragon who Rahm recognized as Kusarn flew down beside the great white dragon. Kusarn was in charge of a small scouting group that followed Lusarth the Black to make sure he stayed neutralized. Kusarn was never to leave his post unless summoned by the King.

In a bellowing voice that demanded respect, the king began, "I am Ranith the White, king of dragons, and I have called for a war gathering!" When he said this, a great uproar rang out. Ranith waited for a moment, but when the noise did not show sign of stopping, he roared again, silencing them.

"We are going to war against Acodia."

Rahm felt his heart skip a beat. He crept forward toward his father. "Your highness, why are we going to war against Acodia?" He whispered.

"Acodia has rashly claimed that we have stolen it's princess, and has aligned itself with Lusarth the Black to wage war against us. Since the princess, the rightful ruler, has disappeared, a dark warlock has taken the throne and has made the decision. We knew this day was coming, and even though the prophesied warrior has not appeared, we must win. I agreed with King Leland decades ago for peace, and Acodia has broken that agreement. They will now face our full wrath." Rahm watched in fear as the all the dragons roared their approval.

"What if the princess were returned to the throne?" Rahm asked over the noise. Ranith turned sharply to him.

"You know where she is?"

Rahm nodded. "She is the only thing stopping the dark warlock from gaining more power."

Ranith was silent for a moment, then spoke. "Bring her here, I wish to speak with her." Rahm felt a burst of hope and flew upward to tell Kara the good news.

Kara leaned forward and grabbed onto Rahm's horns as they flew. She felt the weight of the wyvern tooth dagger at her hip as Rahm flew her past tall pillars of rock. She was still wearing a black, now ruined, mourning dress, but she hoped she could make a good impression on the dragon king. She took a deep breath and watched the clouds fly beneath them. She had quickly come to the conclusion that riding a dragon was very different from riding a griffin.

"Do you really think your father can help me," Kara asked.

"Ranith the White is wise, and just, he will know what to do." Rahm answered.

Kara smiled. "I can't believe it, my luck is finally working!"

Rahm laughed and flew faster, glad he finally could help. When they got to the crater, only a few dragons, including Ranith, remained. Rahm landed softly and bent so Kara could climb off his neck. She dismounted and stared at Ranith with wide eyes for a moment before curtsying deeply.

"You are the princess?" Ranith asked.

Kara nodded. "I am Queen Kara, rightful heir to the throne of Acodia."

Ranith looked down at her, then looked at a dragon behind her and Rahm, and nodded. The red dragon shot forward with unbelievable speed and grabbed Kara around the waist with one claw before leaping into the sky. Kara screamed and Rahm went to fly after them, but Ranith roared.

"Rahm, come here." Rahm quickly went in front of Ranith, feeling torn.

"But your Highness, she's-"

"I know, she's the princess. The warlock wants her dead to regain power, and if he succeeds, we are doomed, so I have chosen to put her somewhere safe."

"No, your Highness, she has gold eyes!" Rahm said quickly. Ranith's eyes widened and he stared at Rahm in shock.

"First, you break my law to not interact with humans. Not just any human, but the princess. Then I find that she, the small, delicate girl, is the one prophesied to save or destroy us!" Ranith sighed. "Leave me."

"But Your High-"

"LEAVE ME!"

Rahm shrunk as his father shouted. His father had always been kind and just, and it was the first time he had ever shown any sign of anger or disappointment at Rahm. Rahm bowed his head and flew into the sky, wondering where he was going to go.

———————

Kara watched as Rahm vaulted into the sky after them, before looking back and landing at the feet of the huge white dragon. She pushed against the dragon's grip, but it was firm.

"Let me go!" She shouted up to the dragon. The dragon didn't respond. She squirmed and shouted again, demanding her release, but again, the dragon did not respond. Then, Kara had a thought. She realized she had her dagger, but a moment later understood that it would do her no good. The hilt wasn't as long as a sword's, so it was stuck underneath the dragon's claw.

For a moment, Kara thought about the difference between her first dragon kidnapping, and this one. She chuckled at herself, thinking of how she had shuttered with fear and how now she was yelling at the dragon.

Kara constantly checked behind her, hoping that at any moment, Rahm would fly to her and rescue her, but she knew it wasn't going to happen. The white dragon had clearly planned it, and he obviously ruled over Rahm.

So she sat and waited. *Once again, I am helpless.* She thought. A roar to her right made her jump and she looked startled at another dragon that flew in beside her. It looked like other dragons, except it had long, smooth, colorful feathers instead of the leather for wings, and it didn't have any horns. Its build was very sleek and streamlined, and its scales were so small, Kara could hardly make them out. Kara also noticed its waist was smaller than any other dragon's she had seen. Smaller feathers also followed along its cheek. She watched in fascination as the orange dragon flew forward with ease, as if it were weightless.

"What are you doing here?" The dragon carrying her asked. The orange dragon looked over lazily.

"Ranith the White sent me," a female voice said. "He thought you could use some help in case you feel tired." She said it in a way that made Kara think she was referencing something. The dragon holding her growled.

"That was once, the little whelp snuck something in my dinner." The orange dragon just shifted its gaze to Kara. Its eyes reminded Kara of a cat's. Lazy, but taking in and judging everything.

"So, why are you so important?"

Kara opened her mouth to talk, but the red dragon growled again.

"We're not supposed to talk to it!"

The orange dragon flew closer to the red one. "Come now Cornon, we're the ones guarding her, why not make a little conversation." It smiled a little as if it were flirting, and the red dragon looked tempted for a moment, before shaking its head and snorting smoke.

"Temptress! You filata! Untrustworthy as a wyvern."

"Come now, we're all dragons." The orange dragon cooed. The red dragon named Cornon snorted again and flew a bit faster.

"What? Filatas *are* just a type of dragon." The filata rolled its eyes and increased its speed effortlessly. "So, why *are* you so special?" She asked again.

Kara heard and felt the red dragon's low growl, and decided to stay quiet. "Come on, you can tell me."

Kara felt strange looking into the dragoness' eyes. It felt like peace and safety.

"I'm Kara," she stated simply.

The dragoness smiled. "My name is Leara."

"We're here," the red dragon interrupted. The dragon began a slow spiral downward, and Kara looked to see they were heading toward a small cave on the ground. The two dragons landed and the red dragon released her above the ground. Kara landed and right when she stood up Cornon pushed her with the back of his claw toward the cave.

Kara could now see that the cave was too small for the dragons to enter, but she could fit while standing up.

"Sit," the male dragon ordered once she was inside. She did what she was told and leaned back against the cave wall. Then, the red dragon laid down, keeping its head in the air, and stared at her.

"What?" Kara asked, somewhat annoyed at his judgemental stare.

"I'm not taking my eyes off of you." Cornon said. Leara scoffed behind him. Kara had heard their conversation in the sky, and made a bold move.

"Because of something that happened last time you were supposed to watch someone." Kara flinched as the red dragon stood and stepped forward quickly, bringing them nose to nose as it snarled at her.

"You don't know anything." The dragon said quietly. Kara stood and stared him right in the eye. For a moment, there was a stand-off. Then, out of the corner of her eye, Kara saw Leara look a bit closer at her, then make a shocked face. She rushed forward stopped right by the red dragon.

"Look at her eyes," she whispered, though Kara could still hear her. The red dragon seemed to focus more on her stern eyes, and then its eyes widened. It stepped back and looked at Leara.

"I'll tell Ranith," she said a moment before launching into the air. Cornon watched Leara for a moment, before glancing back at Kara. Kara had had it. Almost all the dragons she had met (though she knew that wasn't a lot) had made a big deal about her eyes, and she wanted to know why.

"What is so special about my eyes?!" She said, irritated.

The dragon looked at her for a moment, then said, "It's not my place," before turning its back to her. Kara decided, if he was going to try ignore her, she would have to keep his attention. Cornon was sitting a while away, and the cave cut into a small, grey hill. Kara swallowed, built up her courage, then snuck silently out of the cave and up the hill. Once she was on top, she took a deep breath, and was ready to get some answers.

"I can get away," she yelled down. Cornon swung around and looked in the cave before following her voice and seeing her on top of the hill. "I can, and will run, if you don't tell me-" She didn't get to finish. The dragon flew swiftly toward her, grabbed her and dropped her abruptly into the cave, before sitting right in front of her.

"Don't run again," He ordered.

"Then tell me!" Kara shouted back. Cornon looked at her eyes for a second, then turned back around and sat once more, closer this time. Kara let out a muffled scream of frustration then kicked the side of the cave. She sat down with her back against the wall, trying to think of anything she could do. Then, an idea came.

She scooted to the very back of the cave, where she had to kneel to avoid bumping her head, and silently promised her commitment to the idea. She drew her wyvern tooth knife and looked at it a moment, a shiver going through her body about what she was about to do.

"Dragon," she said. Cornon turned and looked into the cave. "Tell me what is so special about my eyes, or else," she brought the blade of the knife to her neck, "they will close and never open again." Cornon tensed and tried to get into the cave, but he was too big.

"Be reasonable," he said desperately.

"I am. Something about my eyes has shocked almost every dragon I meet, I deserve to know why."

Cornon looked at her with fearful eyes. "I will tell you," he said reluctantly, "but you have to give me the weapon first."

Kara thought a minute. Her knife was the only weapon she had. "How do I know that you'll keep your promise?"

"You have my dragon oath." He said it as if it were the highest degree of oaths, so Kara lowered the knife and crawled until she could stand. Once she was at the entrance, Cornon held out a claw, and Kara placed her dagger in his claw. His talons curled around the tooth and he placed it on the ground with his claw over it.

"Now tell," Kara said.

The dragon looked at her wistfully before sighing.

"Sixteen years ago, a woman came to the dragon lands. She told us she came from a land almost completely destroyed by an evil threat. She told us that in time, the threat destroying her land would come to Acodia. We didn't care, until she told us that the threat would align itself with Lusarth. Lusarth would have an army ready. We were told, that the forces would be evenly matched in war, but there would be one, a human warrior with gold eyes, that would tip the scales. She did not say whether or not the warrior would tip the scales for good, or evil, but left us knowing that one person, one person with gold eyes, would be the difference between life or death of an entire civilization."

Kara listened, her eyes growing wider and wider.

"And, you think I'm the human warrior?"

The dragon sighed.

"Unfortunately, yes." Cornon opened his mouth as if to say something more, but it stopped and looked behind it, as if it heard something.

"What is it?" Kara asked.

His eyes grew wide and his head hung slightly, he spoke almost reverently, "The war has begun."

Chapter Twelve

War

Miles away, on the border of the Dragon Lands, two armies stood. On one side, Ranith the White stood at the head of his army, hundreds of dragons and filatas stood behind him, gleaming in shining armour. On the other side of the soon to be battlefield, stood Rogar, beside Lusarth the Black. Lusarth the Black had equipped his dragon soldiers in helmets, battle claws, and blades fit to their wings. Human warriors joined wyverns, other dragons, and filatas as they formed lines. Mounted knights, archers, and even catapults pulled by bulls aided Lusarth's army.

"Foolish brother! You think I would limp away from our last battle and not seek revenge?" Lusarth called across the battlefield.

"No my brother, I had hope that you were smarter than that." Ranith replied.

Lusarth the Black roared in rage. **"YOU WILL SEE TRUE POWER!!** *ATTACK!"*

The dragons and humans standing behind Lusarth surged forward with battle cries that rocked the menacing mountains. Lusarth himself spread his wings and flew forward. Ranith flew forward as well, his legion of dragons flying behind him into battle.

The dragons on either side met, biting, breathing fire, clubbing tails, like a choreographed war dance. Each doing anything they could do to take the dragon, each was fighting, out of the sky. The beauty of the beasts and the rage of war equally matched. The humans soon caught up, and began shooting their bows, and catapults up towards Ranith's army. Dragons fell from the sky, horrible screams of agony filled the air, yet both sides fought on, not willing to relinquish victory.

Lusarth the Black tore through the lines, using his size and speed to his advantage, downing dragons left and right. It was as though he had one purpose in mind. Sometimes they were even his own dragons, but he didn't care, he knew he would win the battle. He had been there for the prophecy, and he knew without the golden eyed warrior, to tip the scales of his enemy, there was no way he could lose this battle. He was sure the prophecy was in *his* favor. Though allies, Rogar still had his own intentions at the forefront of his mind. He was still keeping secrets and weaving webs. Because of this, he had neglected to tell Lusarth that he had found the golden eyed warrior.

Eventually, Lusarth saw his intended target. Ranith the White was helping his troops, fighting valiantly to save his friends and subjects. Lusarth smiled and propelled himself through the air like an arrow at his brother. He rammed into Ranith, sending his foe flying through the air. As soon as the White King recovered, Lusarth flew forward and locked claws with him, spinning and flinging him toward the ground. He lunged forward and bit at Ranith's neck, but the King flew backward, and Lusarth's jaws closed with a snap on empty air. Ranith pulled himself from Lusarth's grasp and turned, hitting Lusarth with his spiked tail. Not knowing what had happened, Lusarth was thrust back from the force of the attack.

"You cannot win. You could not win decades ago, you cannot win today, and you will never win!" Ranith shouted, flying high above his brother.

Lusarth smiled. "Foolish, weak brother!" Lusarth roared.

From the skies below and behind him, dragons from the dark army flew forward and attacked Ranith the White, shredding his wings and staining his white scales red. Two dragons flew forward and grabbed his wings, pinning them to his side. Lusarth watched in pleasure as Ranith fell, unable to catch himself as the two dragons flew beside him, keeping his wings at his side.

"FATHER!" Lusarth turned to see Rahm streaking toward his father, the falling King. He laughed and roared again. His nephew would have other problems. Another one of his soldiers flew forward towards Rahm. Connecting with Rahm from above. The soldier drove his horns into Rahm's horns, sending him horn over tail.

As Ranith the once powerful king, grew closer to the jagged ground below, the two dragons released and pushed down, sending him faster toward the ground.

All at once, the world shook. A thunder filled the air, echoing through everything living, silencing the battlefield. Lusarth dove and landed by his dying brother.

"*Long live Ranith the White*," he shouted mockingly. He raised his head, and brought his teeth down in the final blow. Evil filled his very soul. So much hatred and jealousy coursed through his veins.

"Nooooooooooooo!" Rahm bellowed feeling as though his heart might burst. But it was too late, Ranith the White was dead. Both sides stood still in shock. Lusarth roared at his victory.

"Retreat!" Rahm shouted. "Retreat!" The dragons from his father's army flew back, fear enveloping them.

Lusarth laughed in complete victory. "Let the cowards run, they have nowhere to go, we are victorious!"

A great cheer arose from the winning army.

———————————

Kara could hear roars, heartbroken, terrible roars. She felt something in her bones, something was not right. She and Cornon waited in agonizing silence for what felt like a lifetime. She felt a pit in her stomach as she heard the cries. The feeling was deepening and all consuming. She looked over at the dragon guarding her, and felt the pit widen.

She broke the silence, she could no longer stand it, "What is it?"

The dragon looked at her, his spirit so broken, she could barely stand seeing him.

"Ranith the White has fallen, the battle is lost." The dragon said, his broken soul apparent in his quiet voice. Kara felt a deep aching, then a fire.

"The battle is lost, but not the war."

Cornon looked at her, confused. "What are you talking about?"

"The prophecy said that a gold eyed warrior would tip the scales! I am the gold eyed warrior, let me fight!"

Cornon opened his mouth to argue, but Kara cut him off. "Let me go on the battlefield. Even if I can't fight, I still have to tip the scales. Plus, if my army sees me, they will follow me, so at least you'll have more support. You must summon Rahm, please."

"Rahm?"

Kara swallowed, feeling a deep sympathy for Rahm. "He's the new king."

Cornon looked thoughtful for a moment. "Fine, let's go."

"Go where?" A feminine voice asked behind him.

Kara looked behind Cornon and saw Leara land with a few other dragons behind her.

"Leara! We have a plan," Kara started, moving toward Leara, but Cornon blocked her from taking another step. Kara looked up at him and saw him glaring at Leara. Then it hit her. Leara had returned, after she had said she was going to tell Ranith the White about Kara's golden eyes, but he was dead. Leara was not, instead she returned with dragons, dragons prepared to fight. The easy smile that Leara wore sent chills up Kara's spine.

"A plan? Please tell, what shall we do?" Leara said comfortably. Kara almost wanted to, but she wasn't that stupid. Still, she knew if she didn't speak, there was no way she was getting out of this alive. She climbed up onto the red dragon's back.

"We must go, we will tell you on the way," she said, faking happiness. Cornon didn't need any more encouragement. He took off into the sky.

"What are you doing?" He whispered back to Kara once they were ahead of the other dragons.

"They would have attacked if they suspected anything."

"So now what?" He asked. Kara didn't get to answer. She screamed as she was ripped from Cornon's back, and cold, hard claws wrapped tightly around her.

"Wait!" She heard Cornon shout, but the dragon that had her held onto her tighter. Kara turned and saw Cornon fighting two other dragons, while Leara flew up beside her.

"So, tell me, what was your plan?"

"Your Highness, what do we do?" A dragon asked Rahm. Rahm paced, how could this happen? He was still young, and now he was thrown into this chaotic world.

"Where are my father's advisors?"

"All of them are dead or missing your highness."

Rahm paced even more, thinking as fast as he could. Since they fled, they had not gone to the mountain, they had scattered. Now, Rahm and six other dragons, plus one male filata who was keeping watch outside, were huddled in a large cavern, hiding from Lusarth the Black.

"Someone's coming," the filata yelled, flying into their hiding place.

"Who?" Rahm asked.

"Cornon." The filata answered. Rahm tilted his head, silently asking who that was.

"Your father assigned him to watch the human."

Rahm ran past the filata to the entrance and immediately saw the rust red dragon. He flew crookedly, and Rahm could tell he was injured.

"Where's Kara," Rahm asked as Cornon landed in front of him.

"We were betrayed your highness," he spoke quickly, "Leara found that the girl had gold eyes, she claimed she was delivering the message to your father. We knew the king was dead, and the gold eyed girl convinced me to bring her to you, so she could gain your support in her plan. She wanted to fight, and she made it reasonable, but before we could leave, Leara returned with other dragons, dressed for battle. They stole the girl, I was almost killed. I bested the two and came straight here."

Rahm felt his head spin. "They took Kara?"

"Yes your highness. I did everything I could, but by the time I had taken care of the dragons attacking me, I was weak, and the rest were gone."

"Which way did they go?" Rahm asked, even though he had a creeping feeling that he already knew.

"Toward the mountain." Cornon responded.

Rahm closed his eyes. "Stay here, I will return."

Before anyone could argue, he flew up into the sky, pointing his head to the mountain.

Chapter Thirteen

Capture

Kara stayed silent the entire flight, resisting all urges to reveal everything as Leara continued asking questions.

"Come now, I was your first friend, I just want to help you. If you don't let me help you, who will?" Leara said, her voice so sickly sweet it made Kara want to gag.

"No," she said. It was the first word she had uttered the entire time. "No, you're wrong, Rahm was my first friend. You're lying!"

Leara roared in anger, and Kara was frightened for a moment at the display of rage. But Leara recovered with eerie speed. Kara shook her head, why did she let her anger reveal her friendship with Rahm. She was, once again, determined to remain silent.

"Very well, Lusarth will interrogate you then." Kara felt the color drain from her face. "Ah, here we are!" Leara began spiraling downward, the dragon holding Kara following her lead. Kara looked down and saw their destination. The crater like mountain where she had gone to meet Ranith the White. Now, hundreds of battle clad dragons, wyverns, and filatas sat in the step like seats, staring down in horrible joy as a dragon battled three wyverns at the floor of the cavern.

Dragons were shouting, and yelling, cheering either for the wyverns or the dragon. The dragon burst free from the wyverns' hold and shot upward, desperately trying to escape. As he rose up away from the wyverns, two spectating dragons flew forward and pushed the first down, back into the fight. Kara watched this, disgusted. The dragon in battle was not only outnumbered, but it had no armour, and the wyverns did.

Leara led the way down to a particularly large step, where Lusarth the Black sat, laughing in entertainment at the fight taking place. He had two, large dragons on either side of him, and one stepped forward when they landed.

"Halt! Who are you, and what business do you have with Great Lusarth the Black?"

Leara smiled and continued as if she was completely unaware of the royalty that she was approaching. "It's quite private, but if you'll let me take care of it, I can get a replacement to take your shift and we can talk a bit more." Leara stepped forward, batting her eyes at the dragon.

"That won't work on me, you stupid filata, turn back before I lose my temper."

"Leara?" The dragon king turned, looking past the guard at Leara. "Step aside, good knight, this is my honored colleague." Lusarth strode forward, smiling, until he was in front of Leara. He picked up one of her claws and kissed it as if she was a lady. Kara's stomach turned in anger, sadness, and disgust.

"My dear Leara, trusted partner, jewel of Acodia." Lusarth said sweetly. Kara stared at Lusarth. He seemed so different than when she first met him, or even in her dream. He was more calm, laid back, but still sinister. Leara pulled her claw out of his and rolled her eyes as she turned.

"I'm supposed to be the flattering one, besides, we have urgent news to speak of. Let's go somewhere private."

Lusarth nodded. "Follow me." He spread his wings and flew upward. His guards, Leara, and the dragon holding Kara following him. He flew out of the crater, then down. They glided until Kara saw a ledge sticking out from the otherwise smooth slope. The group landed on the outcropping, and Lusarth turned to one of his guards.

"Take the girl and dismiss the dragon." The guard walked to the edge of the ledge where Kara and the other dragon were.

"I will take the pest from here." Kara fought as she was transferred to the new dragon. "Great Lusarth the Black thanks you for your service" the guard said. Then, he sprang forward and sliced the dragon across the chest with his weaponed wing. The dragon roared in pain, rearing up, before falling backwards off the ledge. Kara watched in horror as one of their own dragons fell, roaring to his death.

"Why?" Kara said quietly in confusion. Leara heard her.

"He knew too much, you can never be too careful."

"Leara," Lusarth said, turning everyone's attention to him. "Did you know, that Ranith kept a hidden passage right here for himself. He was selfish, just like my father, and shared the secret with no one."

Breaking her pledge of silence once again, the words escaped her mouth, "How do you know about it?" Kara asked, daring to question.

"My father told us before he died. He expected us to reign together, that was his mistake." With that, he pressed the mountainside, and a portion of it slid to the side. It reminded Kara of the hidden way out of the castle. Lusarth entered the new hole in the mountain that led to a wide, spacious tunnel. Leara followed him, and the guards walked after her. The tunnel was high, and lined with large torches that sent dancing firelight all across the tunnel. Lusarth continued walking until the tunnel let out into an enormous, vaulted cavern. Lusarth turned. He transformed into a human without warning, in the blink of an eye. He was still large, about seven feet tall with dark hair that hung past his shoulders tied back at the nape of his neck.

"Release the girl, I would like to talk to her in private." The dragon released her, and Kara dropped to the ground. Before she could respond, Lusarth ran forward with inhuman speed and grabbed her wrists.

"Follow me, *queen*." He dragged Kara to the other side of the cavern, where there was a small, wooden door. He quickly opened the door and shoved Kara through. She whirled around and went to fight back, but he caught her hand and pulled in up above her head, lifting her off the ground. She tried kicking, but it was useless. Lusarth dropped her and pushed her onto a stone chair. He grabbed her wrists and locked them into the armrests, then did the same with her ankles to the legs of the chair. She struggled, but to no avail. Shackled, again.

"What are you going to do?" Kara asked accusingly. Lusarth walked around the room, where there were many bottles of different liquids on shelves. He turned to her.

"Everyone wants you, don't they? Rogar to restore his magic and keep his secret, my nephew to win the war, even me, but I have many purposes." He must have seen the worry on Kara's face. "You can relax, I haven't told Rogar I have you, and I won't. You're far too valuable to kill."

Somehow his words did not reassure her in the least.

"I have one question, where is my nephew?"

She remained silent.

"You *will* tell me." His anger returning, Lusarth grabbed a bottle with a green cream inside. He changed his hands into dragon claws before he opened it and scooped some onto his hands. "Do you know what this is? My great grandfather made it, he had quite the reputation for possessing the most drastic torture techniques. He would rub this cream onto his prisoner's forehead, and it would inflict pain like nothing anyone has ever experienced before. But of course, I don't want to physically hurt you *yet*, so I am pleased that this cream only afflicts pain of the mind. Do not worry **princess**, No harm will be done to your body." He stepped forward, reaching out to place the cream on her forehead. He gently rubbed a small amount onto Kara's head with his sharp dragon claws.

Kara screamed. She felt a thousand knives pierce her body as her bones felt as though they were breaking. Nothing was actually happening to her, but the mixture affected her nerves and mind into thinking that she was in extreme agony. Kara didn't how long she sat there screaming, but as she finally calmed down and the pain subsided, Lusarth stepped over to her.

"Ready to cooperate? Where is Rahm?" Kara took a few deep breaths.

All those years of training, her words to her father, her protests that she could handle a kingdom, as the pain subsided, they all coursed into her veins. With all the calm and royalty she could muster, she replied. "Even if I knew where he was, do you really think I would tell you?"

Lusarth frowned, "You are more resistant than I thought, nothing that can't be fixed." He moved forward to apply more cream to her forehead, but then he stopped. He cocked his head toward the door, moving to partially face it. Kara waited and listened, then understood. She could hear fighting outside. Lusarth smiled. "Looks like

I won't need to use this anymore after all. Looks like *you* were all I needed." He released Kara, only to grab her again. His movements were so fast and flawless. She struggled, but Lusarth's grip was like iron.

"Come, let us go greet my nephew." He pushed Kara to the door and opened it, pushing her out first and drawing a sword he had acquired inside the room. As soon as the door opened, Kara had to squeeze her eyes shut against the light. Rahm was flying high in the middle of the cavern, setting fire to everything. The guards dove and rose, avoiding the flames as Leara cowered in a corner. Her attention snapped to Lusarth and Kara as they entered the room. Leara flew low and fast over to them, and spoke hastily.

"He's gone mad! His wrath is taking in everything in its path. It seems that everyone is his enemy. We must leave!"

Lusarth, still in human form, shook his head. "Leave without me, I have a plan."

Leara opened her mouth to argue, but Rahm released a torrent of fire that fell just short of burning the three of them to ashes. Kara fell to her knees, trying to escape the heat, but Lusarth held her forearm. Leara didn't need any more encouragement. She darted for escape, and slipped out unnoticed. Kara watched as one of the dragons who had been fighting Rahm dropped to the floor, dead, and the other still fought with Rahm.

As Kara got a look at Rahm, her eyes widened. His nose was snarled in fury as he snapped and clawed viciously at the guard. He had no friends here, no foes, no reason to contain his wrath. She was his only friend in the cavern and she was willing to die if it meant the end to Lusarth and his wicked kingdom.

Rahm would fly up and dive at the other dragon, throwing his enemy off balance before clubbing him with his spiked tail. After a strong wind of white fire to the dragon, it fell to the floor, bleeding and bruised. Rahm dropped from the sky, landing on the dragon, a fire in his eyes.

"Where is she?!" He shouted at the dragon.

"Oh, nephew, are you looking for this," Lusarth called to Rahm, pulling Kara up and positioning his sword at her throat. Rahm's eyes widened, and his face softened for a moment as he looked at Kara.

"Are you alright?" He asked gently. Lusarth tightened his grip and brought the sword closer to her skin. She breathed in sharply and felt the cold steel touch her bare neck.

"She's fine," Lusarth said, his voice dripping in sarcasm. Rahm's expression hardened.

"What do you want with her? Leave her out of this, it doesn't concern her."

"Oh but that is where you are a fool Rahm. This does concern her in every way. She is the queen of *my* armies' ally. Right now, the human army, *her* army, is ruled by the dark wizard. He fights alongside me in battle. If ever she returns to her kingdom, she will be able to change alliances, and help *you* and *your* army." As he rambled the sword pressed hard against Kara's neck. She could feel her skin bend against the sharp steel. Her mind raced, trying to find a way to escape Lusarth's grasp. He continued on. "If she returns, *in all her goodness*, my own forces will have to fight twice the resistance, which will make conquering this land so much harder. Now, in her absence, the ruling King of Acodia, King Cole, wants her dead - as he is controlled by my wizard friend. Her death guarantees both Rogar's and King Cole's power. Though the wizard's assistance is appreciated, if this wizard becomes more powerful than me, he will try to dethrone me." Lusarth began to sound more and more desperate with every word that escaped his wicked tongue. "So, you see, **everything** revolves around her. *Including you*." With the way he growled the last two words, Kara got chills.

Rahm snorted, watching with his rage boiling inside. "What are you talking about?"

Lusarth lowered the sword just enough to grab something that hung around Kara's neck. He rose his hand again, and the smooth, gold gem at the end of the chain came into view. Rahm gave a small roar of fury and glared at his uncle.

Lusarth smiled, "You have to ask?"

Kara gave Rahm a questioning look, and he looked away. Lusarth laughed behind her, shaking the sword that was still dangerously close to her. "She doesn't even know what it is, does she?"

"Let her go." Rahm demanded again. Kara couldn't stand it anymore, she was completely clueless and at the mercy of one of her greatest enemies. She bowed her head, as if in defeat, then with Lusarth still grasping her wrists, she jerked back, coming in direct contact with Lusarth's head. He stumbled back, relinquishing his grip on Kara. Stunned a bit herself, she ducked under his blade and ran toward Rahm. Rahm immediately surged forward, but Kara heard a roar behind her and turned in time to see Lusarth, in full dragon form, springing toward her with a look of murder in his eyes. She screamed as she realized he would get to her first. Kara rolled just as Lusarth's claw grazed her shoulder blades.

She cried out, looking up in time to see Lusarth land and use his claws to stop his momentum so he could turn to come back for her. Kara could see the look of total hatred in Lusarth's eyes and her blood ran cold. Before Lusarth could move to attack again, Rahm hit him at full speed, knocking him and sending him rolling forward.

Kara scooted back as quickly as she could as the great black dragon came tumbling toward her. Luckily, Rahm flew over, grabbed Lusarth, and pulled him just high enough that he went over Kara. Lusarth quickly regained his balance and flew upward with Rahm on top of him, hitting the ceiling and smashing Rahm.

"Run Kara!" Rahm screamed.

Kara sat, frozen. This had happened before. *"Run Kara!"* Leo shouted in her mind. Kara closed her eyes. She wouldn't run, not this time. When she opened her eyes, she looked around for anything useful to aid in the duel. A few yards from her, she spotted the sword Lusarth had been using. She scooted backward to where it was and picked it up. All the while, the two kings were fighting above. As Kara looked up, she could see who was winning.

Lusarth bashed Rahm again and again with his tail, stopping occasionally to breathe a torrent of black and red fire at his nephew. Kara thought frantically, trying to formulate a plan. Then, it hit her. She quickly rubbed the gem and her thoughts became one with Rahm, her golden eyes glowed and she moved forward with her plan.

"Rahm, fly me out of here, I have a plan!" She whispered urgently. Rahm flew backward to dodge a tail strike, then dove and grabbed Kara, using the speed from his dive to shoot like an arrow through the tunnel. Rahm's thoughts became Kara's, their royalty becoming one. *"Call the dragons."* She heard Rahm's voice say in her mind. Stunned at Rahm's voice in her mind, there was no time to question it. Kara quickly rubbed the gold gem, and thought of all the dragons who were on Rahm's side, summoning them.

"Your King needs you, come and aid him in winning the war," she yelled into the stone, hoping it had worked and they could hear her. She hoped in her heart that the dragons were not weary of battle and might be ready to fight, because good was quickly losing to evil.

Lusarth flew out behind them, and bellowed a roar that sounded like thunder. Kara turned and saw hundreds of dragons rise from the mountain, following their leader. It was as if the mountain had erupted as thousands of warriors answered their master's call. A cloud of black pulsed towards them and the air sounded as though it had a beating heart.

Filatas and wyverns, the fastest fliers, soon overtook Lusarth the Black. Kara saw Leara in the front of the hoard, gaining rapidly on them.

"Rahm, LOOK OUT!" Kara screamed, but it was too late. A pale green wyvern slashed down from above, slicing Rahm across the shoulder. Rahm whirled in the air, falling quickly, his grip on Kara loosening until she slipped from his claws. She was freefalling. Dragons swooped down, attacking Rahm as he fell upside down. "Rahm!" Kara screamed as they grew closer and closer to the ground. Rahm looked over, then down, his eyes widening. He flipped in the air on purpose, shaking his attackers momentarily, before spreading his wings and swooping forward to catch Kara.

He spread his wings wide, trying to stop the fall, but when it became clear there was no stopping, he curled in his wings as tight as he could, ducking his head in, creating from his wings, a shield around his head and Kara. He pressed Kara tightly against him, but she still jerked and bumped as they collided with the ground. Kara clung to his claw as her body was tossed like a rag doll.

Eventually, it all stopped, and Rahm unfurled his wings to stand, still holding Kara tightly in his claw. He gently set her down, and she wobbled before falling to her knees and looking back at him. His glittering blue scales were stained in dark red blood mixed with dirt. His blood. Out of breath, and grateful to be breathing at all, Kara stood to inspect his wounds, but dragons landed around them, forming a circle of sneering, furious faces. Lusarth landed in front of the rows and rows of dragons forming a circle around Rahm and Kara. Rahm bent a wing and pulled Kara closer, snarling, his mouth already filling with white fire from within.

"Well nephew, it looks like this is it." Lusarth the Black said smugly. Kara looked fearfully from Lusarth to Rahm, then to the sky. She smiled and walked confidently forward, even though she was bruised from head to toe, she knew she had the upper hand.

"Not yet. You forgot something." Kara spoke softly but with confidence.

Lusarth smiled, leaning forward. "And what is that?"

Kara pointed to the sky. "Them."

Chapter Fourteen

The Battle to be Won

Lusarth looked up and behind him just as the first dragons of Rahm's army attacked. Lusarth roared in anger as dragon after dragon of his army were taken by surprise on every side. Every dragon on the ground launched into the air to gain alertness, but Rahm's army was too close already, and many dragons went down before they knew what hit them. Lusarth watched in fury as his unsuspecting, once victorious army became easy targets. Rahm took the opportunity and jumped forward to grab Kara before joining his dragons in the air.

Lusarth looked back to the spot where they had been a moment after they took flight. He let out a monstrous sound that was more a scream than a roar. He leapt into the air, killing any dragon close to him, not caring whose side they were on as he struck them down.

As Rahm and Kara gained altitude, Kara saw a cloud of dust on the horizon. She immediately knew it was a human army.

"Rahm, take me to the dust," Kara said, pointing to the location. Rahm nodded, then weaved through the battle to get closer to the approaching army. Instead of leaving the present battle, it seemed to move with them, until everyone, even the new army, was involved in the battle.

"Get me on your back!" Rahm moved Kara to his back and swooped past a launched boulder to the front lines.

"Acodians!" Kara shouted over the battle. "I am Kara, rightful heir to the throne! Rogar and Cole are traitors to the throne, open your eyes to the real enemy and help me win this war! Shoot down the dragons with the black emblems!" Kara's speech was cut short as a dragon attacked Rahm, rocking her as she fought to hang onto Rahm's back.

"Rahm, let me down on the ground, let me fight with my people!" Rahm dodged an attack, swooped, and deposited her on the ground amid her troops.

"Stay alive," He said before returning to the air. Kata turned to the soldier closest to her.

"Give me a sword!" The foot soldier nodded and handed her one of his extra swords. When she turned back to the battlefield, she saw that Lusarth's dragons had figured out that the humans weren't on their side anymore, and were now landing, destroying the catapults and killing the knights. Kara ran forward to attack one of the destructive dragons, ducking under a blast of fire and jumping onto its back. The dragon immediately felt her and turned its head, but Kara held onto his horns, making it impossible for it to see her. She raised her sword, closing her eyes in preparation for what she was about to do. With one swift movement, she plunged it into the dragon, and instantly it fell. As it collapsed, Kara jumped, landing hard on the ground. She felt sick with guilt at the thing she had just done, but that left her as soon as she heard a voice.

"Hello princess." Kara bolted to a standing position and saw Cole and Rogar standing behind her. The battle raged around them, but no one paid her any attention.

"Traitors." Kara said, her voice full of hatred and anger. There was a roar behind them and Kara turned to see Rahm battling with Lusarth. They danced in the air, circling each other as they exchanged torrents of fire and attacks with clubbed tails and razor sharp claws.

"Oh princess, you should know, this was planned from the beginning. Since you were a baby, I have been planning, waiting, and finally, putting my plans into action for quite some time. I made Cole the knight he is, I made the bull for him to defeat. I made your father sick to hasten his decision as to who you would marry. I made a pact with Lusarth and he sent dragons to attack the countryside. And when not enough dragons volunteered to attack the castle, I controlled them to force the dragons to attack the castle. There are so many things I have done-." He was so pleased with himself. Kara screamed in anger and ran forward, sword raised. She had listened to each thing he had done and her anger burned brighter and brighter until she could not hear one more thing.

Rogar stepped back and Cole stepped in front of him, his sword ready. Kara came crashing down with her sword and Cole moved to the side, easily dodging the attack. Dragons roared all around, there were shouts and screams, growling and moaning. Kara slashed as hard and fast as she could, but Cole just continued moving out of the way.

"Just get it over with!" Rogar commanded. Cole smiled, stepping toward Kara suddenly. Kara, surprised, took a step back and leaned, thinking he was going to attack. She stuck her blade out in front of her, but Cole moved around it, grabbed its hilt, then placed a hand on her shoulder and pushed. Off balance as she was, Kara let go of the sword and fell back. Cole spun her sword in his hand and looked down at her.

"Traitor!" She screamed. At that moment, she saw Cole falter. His smiled faded in a second, as if he was realizing something. Rogar's magic was pulsing through his veins yet it was as though there might still be a hint of a human soul deep within. Then, she knew how she could stop him. "Look around Cole, look at all these people. You allowed Rogar to use you, and now we are at war with a dark force we can't beat." Cole looked around silently, taking in the carnage of battle.

"Cole, you swore to me, I own you!" Rogar desperately yelled, walking up beside him. "Were any of these people there when you were starving alone with your mother? No! You owe them nothing, you owe me *everything*!" Cole looked down at the swords in his hands. Rogar, still fuming, looked past Kara and smiled. Kara turned and cried in fear.

Rahm was still battling Lusarth, but he was losing. Kara could hear Rogar continue talking to Cole, but everything was muffled. She saw Rahm, his shining blue scales smeared with blood, as he barely dodged attack after attack. He began sagging in the air, his head down in exhaustion. Kara stood and started running for him, but Cole grabbed her arm and held her tight. She whirled to see him standing there, his face grim, and Rogar standing behind him.

"You will watch us win our victory, then I will regain my powers." Rogar said, thinking his victory was imminent.

Kara turned away and watched helplessly as Rahm dove again and again, each time rising a little less but still valiantly trying in his attempts to live and win. Lusarth the Black roared, blasting Rahm with a torrent of deep red fire. Kara watched the flames engulf him, screaming.

"Rahm!" Rahm fell out of the flames, accelerating toward the ground. Kara knew he was dead. As he hit the ground, everything went quiet. The fighting stopped, and everyone turned to Lusarth as the ground shook and he roared his victory. Rogar laughed, and something snapped inside of Kara. She felt a fury like never before. Cole let go of her and she turned to see him backing away. She felt wind gather around her, and her body started to change. She closed her eyes and bent her head, feeling a prickling all over her body. Her heart ached, and her fury fed the change.

She felt her body grow, her hands became larger, sharper. She felt wings sprout from her shoulder blades, and claws form at the end of her hands. Her mouth became long, and full of razor sharp teeth, and a crown of regal, beautiful horns extended from her head. Spikes followed down her spine, and a short spurt of fire escaped her lips. When she opened her eyes, she found herself looking down at Cole, a look of absolute terror on his face. She looked at herself, and found she was a dragon. A gleaming, gold, fearsome dragon. She spread her magnificent wings and yelled to the sky, her yell coming out as a great roar. Each from Rahm's army straightened and seemed to lift their heads yet bow at the same time. She turned toward Lusarth, he was flying in the sky half a battle field away, despite the distance, she could clearly see a look of shock on his face. A fearsome roar rolled across the battlefield as she rushed forward in a storm of fury, pounding her wings to lift into the sky with freedom she never knew possible. With her wings, she rapidly closed the distance between herself and Lusarth. Lusarth still held by his shock, not yet processing the event taking place, never saw the mid-air collision coming. Kara propelled herself at his chest with every ounce of her being.

He tumbled through the air, recovering with chilling speed. Kara circled around and breathed spurts of white and blue fire at him. Lusarth wrapped his wings like a shield around himself, blocking the flames. He snapped his wings out, dispersing the heat around him. He growled and flew forward, his claws extended. Kara tucked her wings in, trying to fly under his attack, but he grabbed her from behind, sinking his claws into her scales. She cried out, flipping in the air and shaking off Lusarth's claws.

"So you *are* the one destined to save them?" Lusarth called, his voice savage. Kara flew up and faced him, hovering in the air, a look of absolute hatred on her face.

"Yes, I am." Her voice regal and echoing through the air. She launched forward, her head bent so she could ram him again. Lusarth smiled and flew up and ran his claws along her back as she flew under him. Roaring in pain, and nearly falling out of the sky, she growled, losing blood rapidly. Kara turned and looked, seeing that all fighting around her had stopped, everyone staring at the battle between her and Lusarth. She felt a surge of not only anger, but pride. She would **not** let Lusarth and Rogar win. Evil would not fill these lands victoriously today. Her heart beat so hard, she felt that it might burst out of her chest. Warmth filled her chest, and continued to rise to her throat. Lusarth looked at her, and for the first time, she saw fear in his dark red eyes.

Without another thought, a blast of white and blue fire erupted like a volcano from her jaws. Massive surges of flames exploded forward, engulfing Lusarth. Kara could hear him roaring, but continued feeding the fire inside of her. More and more flames lit up the battlefield, Kara had never seen so much fire, never from her own being. She continued staring, her chest filling with more and more, the flames so bright causing everyone to shield their eyes as none dared look away. Then, as the last licks of fire escaped her jaws, Kara closed her mouth, stopping the destructive fire. Lusarth was gone. Turned to a falling shower of ash, Kara couldn't even find a single scale. The battlefield remain still, as if in shock, as Kara, completely spent from the battle, half glided half fell to the ground.

As she collapsed, exhausted and near dead, she felt herself shrink, her claws forming hands and fingers, her wings folded and disappeared into her back, and her horns shrunk and were replaced by a mass of brown hair. She sat up slowly, still weak, and sighed a breath of relief as she looked down and saw she was still wearing her clothes. She looked around, taking no more than a second to locate Rahm's fallen body. Her legs shook and stumbled as she ran to Rahm. He lay on the ground, his wings sprawled to either side of him, his eyes closed.

"Rahm," Kara whispered when she reached him. Kneeling down by his head, seeing the scratches and blood running down his scales, she spoke softly, "Rahm, please answer me." With all the events of the day, surely wishing Rahm alive could not be impossible. She could see he was breathing, but barely. Kara wrapped her arms around his neck right behind his horns. Then, she cried. Great sobs wracked her body as she cried onto his scales, sobbing like a child as she closed her eyes. Tears for all she had lost in her short life. Her mother, father, Leo; those she loved most dear. Rahm's name could not be added to that list.

"Don't die, please don't," she begged him. "I've had too many others, you can't die too. You can't leave me alone to deal with this place. Your kingdom needs you, and I need you. Don't die Rahm." She pleaded, she made outrageous promises, her tears falling onto his scales. The entire battlefield watched, still shaken from the scene that unfolded just moments before. She felt so alone, the thousands surrounding her disappeared and it was just the two of them, as if they were back in his cave before this whole nightmare unfolded. She stopped and stayed still, not moving, feeling his neck expand and shrink as he breathed. Then he moved. Kara slowly opened her eyes in surprise, wondering if she had really felt him move, wondering if she were dreaming. Then he moved again, just a little. Kara let go and almost jumped back, staring at Rahm in awe.

Rahm moved his legs under himself and pushed, standing up as he pulled his head off the ground. He opened his eyes, his legs shaking beneath him. He turned his head to look at Kara as she knelt on the muddy ground, her tears having made streaks of clean on her dirty face.

"I told you dragons heal fast." Was all he said. Kara stared at him a minute longer, then a huge smile broke out across her face as tears washed it clean.

"Great, now that you're awake, I can relax." With that, Kara closed her eyes, and passed out.

———————

"Kara, Kara?" Kara heard her name and Rahm's voice, but her eyelids were like lead.

"She'll be fine, I'm almost positive." Kara opened her eye just enough to see that she was in her room again, and a physician was talking to a young man with brown hair and silver eyes. Rahm. The physician glanced over at Kara and smiled.

"Looks like she will make it." Rahm followed his gaze and Kara could see relief fill his face as their eyes met. He turned and walked over to her.

"Are you okay?" He asked.

"What kind of a question is that? I have wounds head to toe, I hurt inside and out, not to mention I just barely survived one of the worst battles in history!"

Rahm chuckled. "Good to see you haven't changed."

Kara went to sit up, but black dots speckled her vision and she felt a hand push her back down.

"You've lost a lot of blood, you should take it easy for a while." The physician said. Kara nodded, accepting a glass of water that the physician held out to her. She downed it in one long gulp, feeling better already. Then a few things came to mind.

"Where are Rogar and Cole?" She asked, her voice deadly. Rahm frowned, his forehead creasing.

"Rogar tried to kill you as soon as you fainted, sending Cole forward to end you. I got to Cole first, and threw him aside. I killed Rogar; his power was fading very quickly and he tried to block me with spells to no avail. Once he was dead, Cole shrank and became a scrawny boy too weak to even lift the armour he was wearing. It didn't seem right to kill him while he was like that, without Rogar he is not much of a threat. So I banished him. I sent two dragons, whom I deeply trust, to make sure he gets across the border. They're gone."

Kara closed her eyes, at peace knowing all the wrong evil had created was avenged. She relaxed for the first time in months, knowing she was safe at last. A deep and dreamless sleep came over her, and she welcomed it.

It took a week for her to recover back to her full strength. All were surprised just how quickly she recovered. She blamed her own resilience. Rahm, who had no knowledge of her transformation during the battle, joked that it was from her dragon side. They finally ended the dispute when they agreed that, whatever caused the rapid healing, it was good.

Kara looked at herself in the mirror. The royal seamstress circled her to look at the dress that she had made. The noble, cool blue, silk dress flowed from top to bottom and had a circle neckline, which subtly revealed the stylish white dress worn below it. The fine corset of her dress hugged tightly to her bodice where the continuous flow was broken up by a thin silver belt worn low around her waist. Below the ribbon the dress opened up left and right and revealed the white dress below. The blue silk flowed freely behind her. The sleeves were purposely too long and flowed over her hands. Two, small silver cloth bands went over the sleeves just below the shoulder.

Her light brown hair was curled, the front pulled back from her face in braids. The back had a single braid where the two front ones met that fell down her back with the rest of her curled hair. Her crown, which had been recovered, was placed gently between the two front braids, the gold and silver shining brightly as if glowing. Kara's face had been powdered a lighter shade and her lips stained a brighter red. She wore the necklace with the gold gem Rahm had given her. The seamstress gave it one last look, then nodded her approval. Kara looked into the mirror, taking in a deep empowering breath, knowing that she was now queen of a whole country. A country who was in desperate need of an anchor of strength.

Her breath lifted her head and pulled back her shoulders, and with one last glance in the mirror, she walked out of the room. Two guards in armour stood outside her door and escorted her to the courtyard. She knew that, usually for occasions like this, it would have been done in the throne room, but she not only wanted to address her people, but the dragons as well. She walked onto a raised wooden platform that had been constructed so that she and Rahm could stand side by side, even in his true form, and be seen by most of the audience.

Rahm was already there, standing straight and tall as a dragon, looking as royal as a king. Kara came and stood by him, trying her best to look like a queen.

"My people," she said, speaking loud enough that both the dragons and people in the courtyard could hear her. As the sun shone down, she felt her mother by her side. "We have faced many trials, many hardships. Our kings have been taken from us in a time of need, and both of our kingdoms have been part of a terrible war. Yet *we have* prevailed! We have conquered our trials, together! I believe that we, as one, can rebuild our country."

"Dragons no longer need to fear humans, and humans no longer need to fear dragons." Rahm spoke. "We all have at least one thing in common. Acodia is our home. It is time that we put our differences aside, and we live in peace together. Our land has been ravaged by a terrible war, but we can, and will rebuild!" The crowd cheered, and the dragons roared. For too long there had been fear of each other, and now, almost everyone was looking forward to a time of peace.

Kara smiled at her people, knowing that the danger was over. She sent a glance over to Rahm, who was also grinning at the approval. He looked older now, if that was possible. He stood a bit taller, a bit stronger. It was as if becoming king had matured him. Kara knew how it felt. Rahm caught her looking at him and his smile grew. He leaned toward her just enough so she could hear him over the cheers.

"Meet me outside the walls by the stables before sunset." Kara could barely hear him, and wondered for a moment whether she had actually heard him or imagined it. Since the battle, they hadn't had much time to together, and she was excited by the idea of getting to talk like old times. She briefly wondered if they were going back to the cave, but then realized there was no need now. The world was right again.

It took a while after the speech to convince her new personal guards to leave her alone, but eventually, after she reminded them that she could turn into a dragon, she chuckled at the very thought. With that reminder, they nodded and left. Kara waited in her room for a few minutes, then, picking a dark brown cloak from her closet, she walked out of her room. She walked with her head down and her hood up, trying to get by without anyone recognizing her. The servants and maids walked around her, no one sending even a second glance at her. Kara walked to the stables, knowing she could make it beyond the walls by using the moving wall.

A pang of sadness caught her off guard as she the thought of the moving wall, memories flooding her mind, reminding her of one of her closest friends. Leo. He had been the one who had told her about the wall. She wondered where his body was, had anyone ever found it? She bowed her head in thought, closing her eyes as she remembered when everything was simple.

Quickly, her mind came to the present, and she stopped, realizing that she was standing at the wall. Kara pressed on the cold stones, watching as one gave way to the outside of the wall. She walked out, looking around. As the wall went back into place, she heard a laugh. She spun around to see Rahm, his blue dragon scales shining as he stood, rubbing his nose with his claw. She realized that the wall must have hit him when she came out. Kara curtseyed deeply.

"Your highness," she said, assuming a royal voice. She glanced up, unable to contain a small smirk. Rahm laughed again, and this time, Kara joined him.

"Why did you want to meet here?" Kara asked, still smiling, after they had finished laughing.

Rahm looked at her a moment with an unreadable expression. "I just had a few questions."

Kara sat down, preparing for what she thought would be a long talk. "Ask away."

Rahm looked around. "Could we do it somewhere else?"

Kara tilted her head in question, trying to think of somewhere they could go. Then she remembered a place. "I know a nice hill, not too far from here." She remembered it from when she had run to ask Rahm for a griffon the first time.

Rahm lowered his neck so she could get on. She pulled up her skirts so she could ride easier, then told him which direction he should go. It was a short flight, but Kara enjoyed every minute. When they landed, Kara slid off, landing nimbly on her feet. They walked up the small grassy hill, the long, green grass waving slowly at their feet.

Kara smiled as she reached the top. She could see humans and dragons, rebuilding and interacting, all around them. At last, their land was at peace. The sun was warm, the crisp breeze playing with strands of Kara's hair. The beauty of the moment captivated both of them for a moment, and Kara wanted to absorb as much of it as possible. Finally, her curiosity got the best of her.

"What did you want to know?" Kara asked. Rahm made that unreadable face again, and Kara almost thought it was regret.

"What happened after I fell," he asked.

"What?"

"When Lusarth knocked me out of the sky, everything went black. What happened?"

Kara sat there for a moment, wondering how it was possible; had no one told him? She knew the answer and started blushing, twirling a piece of hair with her finger.

"I killed Lusarth." She said quietly. Rahm looked at her, stunned for a moment.

"How?"

"I," Kara paused, "turned into a golden dragon."

Silence filled the air as Rahm sat wondering, contemplating the meaning of her words. How could this be possible? The silence lingered a bit longer as Kara sat waiting for a reaction.

"I don't understand. You can turn into a dragon?!"

Kara took a deep breath. "That was the first time. And, I think it was the last. I haven't been able to change since." The hairs on the back of her neck stood up and when she looked over at Rahm. He was in his human form again, standing beside her. He reached down for her hand, then helped her stand up. Kara stood, and instead of letting go of her hand, Rahm picked up her other hand.

"What are you doing?" She asked. She watched, amazed, as Rahm slowly changed, his hands becoming larger and sharper. But that wasn't what amazed her. What amazed her was the fact that her hands were changing too.

"Focus," Rahm said, talking to himself as much as he was talking to Kara. Kara closed her eyes, fearing the flames and the fury that she had felt when she changed before. It took her a moment, but she found that it wasn't her fury that fueled the change, but a desire within her heart. She felt her body grow once more. The process was quicker this time, and Kara felt the change in a matter of seconds. When she opened her eyes, she knew she was a dragon again. She looked over at Rahm, who was also in dragon form, and found him gaping at her, his eyes wide. She felt that somehow, even with her scales, her cheeks were bright red.

"What?"

"I almost didn't believe you." He said in awe. Kara smiled timidly and changed back into a human. She felt the hairs on the back of her neck stand up again, and turned to see Rahm once again a human. She ran her fingers back through her hair, almost feeling the horns that had replaced it moments ago. As Kara dropped her hand from her hair, her fingers brushed the gem Rahm had given her. That made her think of a question.

"Rahm, when Lusarth was holding me captive, he mentioned something about this necklace being special. And when we were fleeing, I was able to call to other dragons to help, why?"

Rahm looked away, and Kara could tell he was debating whether or not to tell her. "Please Rahm, I'm done with being left in the dark."

Rahm sighed. "It's a tradition for each royal heir to make a betrothal necklace for his mate. If the queen, or rather his betrothed, is ever in danger, she can always think of her subjects or any one dragon and contact help." Kara was so shocked, she couldn't do or say anything.

"I just couldn't think of any other way for you to contact me, it doesn't mean that, I mean..."

Kara suddenly felt very wrong for wearing it, she went to take it off.

"Do you want it back?" She asked, uncertain as to what to do.

"No, no, it's okay. You can keep it, just in case you ever need help." Rahm said lowering her hands. Kara blushed. She turned toward the sunset, the dragons flying over the villages reminding her of their new alliance.

"I guess we rule together now?" It was more a question than a statement, and Kara breathed a sigh of relief when she saw Rahm nod.

"We'll rule in peace and see where the future takes us." Rahm said, hope for the future clear in his voice.

Kara turned and smiled at Rahm.

"I like the sound of that."

THE END

Made in the USA
San Bernardino, CA
04 December 2017